ANGEL
IN THE
MIDST

Best Wishes
Laura McClure

LAURA McCLURE

authorHOUSE®

AuthorHouse™
1663 Liberty Drive
Bloomington, IN 47403
www.authorhouse.com
Phone: 1-800-839-8640

Published by AuthorHouse 10/06/2014

ISBN: 978-1-4969-4466-5 (sc)
ISBN: 978-1-4969-4467-2 (hc)
ISBN: 978-1-4969-4465-8 (e)

Library of Congress Control Number: 2014917898

This book is dedicated to my angel in heaven Michelle Renae McClure who died October 19, 2007 of HIV-AIDS complications and to all who have suffered or lost someone to this disease. I pray that through Research that a cure for this disease will soon be found and through education ignorance of the disease will no longer prevail.

ACKNOWLEDGMENTS

I want to give thanks to my heavenly father who gives me life and the desire to reach for my dreams. To my mother and father Mr. and Mrs. Isom Martin and my brother Harold S Martin, who now resides in heaven for all the love and care you gave to me. To my sisters Loretta and Tina who love me and encourages me to be better. To all of my Grandchildren, David, Derrick, Kimberly, Andrew, DeAndre, Michael, Darius, Angelique, Fred, Ariel, Shalette, Ciara, Kristin, Morgan, Brandon and Danny. To my Great grand kids, Cameron, Laila, Sydney, Peyton, Champion, Brooklyn, Michael, Mason. You guys make my life a joy to live.

To my son, Pastor Fredrick and Marilyn McClure, I would like to thank you for the 22 years you were my pastor, always giving me encouragement and joy. You always told me what I needed to hear, not just what I wanted to hear. To my son Pastor Michael and Angela McClure, for all the laughter and joy you gave to me, for always being able to make me laugh no matter what the situation was. To Pastor Roderick and Teri McClure, who pushed me and would not ever allow me to give up on me. Who listen, gave advice on this project and supported me all the way. To My girls, Sharon McClure Olds and Cara McClure Black, you guys are my heroes. You young women showed me what courage really is. How to not let nothing stop you from being the best that God would have you to be.

My Angel Michelle, who left me way too soon. I can still hear you telling me, "You can do it mama if you put God first. I will always love you Michelle and yes you were right I can do all things through Jesus Christ who strengthens me."

Danny, Brandon, Derrick, Morgan, and Kristin, you guys think that I can do anything. I love the respect and the love that you guys feel towards me. You do not know Morgan how good it made me feel when you said I am so proud of you Grandma. I love this family so much.

To my good friend Donna Plummer, who worked with me, encouraging me, giving me solid advice, and correcting my punctuations and grammar. Thank you Donna for your time and effort and not being afraid to tell me what I needed to know. I heard everything you said. I appreciate all of your advice.

To my Pastor now. Pastor Darius McClure, you instilled in me To Think Big and Never Give Up. To Speak Life over me and my work. I thank you for your encouragement.

To all at Author House who has worked with me on this book, I thank and appreciate you.

To everyone that buys this book I appreciate you so much. I would love to hear from you and I thank all of you that is helping me to tell others about this book. May God bless and keep all of you.

Laura McClure
McClurelmc@gmail.com

There comes a time in life when you start wondering, is this all life holds for me? When did I stop dreaming and planning? All I have to do is wait—but wait on what? I do not know. Then something or someone comes along and that spark you once felt comes alive, and you can see yourself doing more and being more. You look in the mirror and do not recognize the face that is staring at you. The eyes look alive, and deep in your soul you know that it is not over for you.

This is what happened to the women in this story. In a beauty shop of all places, six women became very good friends—and one of them, named Brandi, who was a stripper, changed their lives forever. She showed them that it was not over for her, and she took them along for the ride.

She became their *Angel in the Midst*.

Devin was the owner of the beauty shop and was in her early fifties. Actually, she'd turned her basement into a salon. Five women came there every Thursday at three p.m. to get their hair done—Lori, Helen, Yvonne, Christine, and Brandi. These women had become good friends, and Devin really loved working with them. They talked about everything in that shop. What you said at Devin's stayed at Devin's, just like Vegas.

Lori was fifty-six years old and general manager of the largest hotel in the city. Separated from her husband, she seemed to have everything going for her, but she wanted more for herself. She wanted to give up her great job and move out of state, just start all over. There were so many in the company who wanted her job. She couldn't trust most of the people she worked with. There was so much pressure to stay on top of everything.

It was rare for a woman—and especially a woman of color—to have her position. However, Lori was at the top of her game. She knew the hotel industry, and she'd worked her way from the bottom up. She'd met some of the biggest names in show business and politics. She had great friends all over the country. She'd had presidents and their families as guests in her hotel. She'd earned this job, and she would leave it on her own terms, not because someone else schemed and got it.

However, would she have the courage to uproot her life and move on? That's the question she was asking herself over and over. *Can I make this move? Do I have the courage to start over?*

Helen was a beautiful woman in her early thirties. She was the personal secretary to one of the top executives at the power company. For a second time, she had found herself in a failing marriage to an abuser and a womanizer. She was afraid to leave. She just could not get it right with men. She had not yet learned that she did not need a man to validate her. Her professional life was good, but her personal life was another story.

Yvonne was in her thirties, attractive, married, and working in corporate America. She was senior vice president of Brown's Service, a carrier company ranked third in the industry. Yvonne was a sexually frustrated woman and a moral snob. Everything was a sin to her. Even talking about sex was a sin to her. Her marriage had real problems. She had no children. In spite of her success and her marriage to a successful, loving man, Yvonne was very unhappy. She was also a secret drinker—though not enough to get *drunk*, of course, because being drunk was a sin.

Christine, called Chris for short, was the widow of the group in her late forties. Divorced from her first husband, she remarried only to have the second husband die in his sleep. She jokingly said that he died with a smile on his face.

Her husband left her well off, and she now owned her own printing business. Money was no problem for her. However, she was looking for something. She thought she could find it with young lovers and a bag of grass. However, was it working for her?

Brandi was a twenty-eight-year-old single mom who had already lived three lives. She was a high-achieving student in college, doing very well, but something happened to her there that she had shared with no one. The experience robbed her of her confidence, her focus, and her drive. Consequently, she left school and became a stripper. She found religion through a street evangelism program but later found that there was no assurance of money and fame in religion, so she went back to dancing. Later on, she met and married a drug dealer who abused her and made her help in the drug business. Now, divorced, she was back to dancing again.

Her viewpoint on any subject could be very harsh. Brandi trusted very few people. However, she found herself drawn to the women who met at the salon. Brandi felt comfortable with these women and she knew that she wanted them in her corner. She was always glad to be in their company. Brandi really looked forward to Thursday's at Devin's.

CHAPTER 1

I am taking the day off, Lori thought to herself as she woke up. *I am tired with a capital T and looking forward to an evening at the beauty shop. I am going to call Henry, my assistant, and tell him to handle the day and please do not disturb me at all. He wants the job, and today he can act as if it is his and handle it. I can just see him now running all over the place being important.*

She knew that all of the regulars would be at Devin's. She was really looking forward to being in the shop with her friends. There was something on her mind, and she wanted to talk to the women about it and hear what they thought of what she was planning. She knew that she would get a variety of comments and advice.

She'd had this dream for a long time. She knew that now was the time for her to act on it. Life was not yet over for her. She still had plenty of time to conquer a completely new world for herself, and she planned to do just that.

This has been one crazy day, thought Helen. *I cannot think straight. My nerves are really on edge. One problem after another. My head is throbbing.* She was beginning to feel like someone in the office was trying to sabotage her. Over $60,000 in invoices was missing. She'd personally checked those invoices and entered them into her computer. Someone in the office either didn't understand how to use the software or was trying to make her look bad. She couldn't settle the account without those invoices.

Clearly, she needed to find out who had gained access to her computer. *Time to change all of my passwords, too. In fact, let me do that right this minute. If I have to keep going through this, heads are going to start rolling.* This was the third time this month this had happened. She was beyond ready to move on to something new in her life.

Lord, when will this day be over? She was really looking forward to her three p.m. appointment at the beauty shop. She could really use some pampering, and she wanted to see all the girls. Conversation might be heavy today, and that was always interesting. They could always count on Christine to have lots to say. Her conversations were always hot and heavy.

Helen took one last look at the clock on the wall and thought to herself that time had stopped and three o'clock would never come. She turned her attention to another problem.

Brandi had worked late the night before. The club was jumping, and she didn't leave until she'd made all the tips she could get. Now, she knew she had to get up and get herself ready to go to the salon. At least she had someone to come in to clean and cook for her and her son on Thursdays so she could get to the shop.

She loved being around those women. Although they were older, she could teach some of them a thing or two about men—Yvonne in particular. Christine did not need any help in the men department. That woman was just plain man crazy and did not care who knew it. Brandi laughed to herself as she thought about Christine and how she tortured poor Yvonne with all of her sex talk.

Christine was having a good day, and she was looking forward to getting to Devin's with the gang. She had gotten two new accounts for her business, and all of her clients were paying on time. This was the best month for her company revenue-wise this year. She could do no wrong.

She wanted to tell her salon friends all about her social life. She loved making Yvonne feel uncomfortable with all of her young-person sex talk. She laughed to herself. What a prude that Yvonne was, but she liked the woman very much. Yvonne just needed to lighten up some and stop preaching to everybody all the time.

Wait until she hears what I have to tell them today. It will make her hair curl. Christine laughed as she thought of things to say to make Yvonne squirm.

Yvonne really looked forward to Thursdays. Her life was quiet and dull. She enjoyed hearing about what was going on with the rest of the women. True, Christine embarrassed her with all of her talk about young men and sex—it was downright sinful the way that woman talked. However, she had to admit that she wanted to know what was going on with the girl.

I really wish something exciting would happen for me, Yvonne thought. *I would love to see them all eager to hear my news of the day. However, the way things are in my life, it just seems that I am waiting on something, but I have no idea what that something is. Oh well, soon it will be time to be on my way to Devin's. I will not let Christine get under my skin today. If I can get the others to not listen to her, then maybe she will behave herself.*

Devin had gone to the beauty-supply store and purchased what she needed for her Thursday clients. She decided to get some snacks for the women. She made herself busy preparing the snacks and putting out magazines. She wanted everything ready when they all arrived. No one would be reading, but she thought the magazines made the place look more like a beauty shop.

She had converted her basement into a makeshift salon. The women who were coming today were her special clientele. Every Thursday, just like clockwork, they arrived, with no idea that they were her *only* clients. All of her other clients had left to go to the big fancy salons around town.

Devin did not mind that at all. She was not in a financial bind, and she only wanted these women to come. They were more like sisters than clients. She looked up at the clock and saw that it was almost 3 p.m. She knew the women would be coming through that door any moment now. A few of them had called and said they would be a little late today. However, she knew they wouldn't miss their weekly ritual.

Lori was the first of the gang to arrive at the shop. She was disappointed that none of the others had gotten there yet. Devin just laughed and told her they were coming and all of them were running late.

Devin knew that Lori loved being at the shampoo bowl for a long time. Getting her hair shampooed always relaxed her. As Devin was massaging the shampoo into her hair, the conversation started.

Devin asked, "What is going on with you, girl? Anything new?"

That is all it took for discussion to start. It was on for now, and the rest of the gang would have to catch up.

"Well, Devin, I am thinking about moving to Atlanta," Lori said. "I see no reason why I should not make the move. All of my children are grown and have their own lives to live. I am separated from my husband, and I have always wanted to live in Atlanta. I feel this is the right time."

Devin was surprised that Lori wanted to move to Atlanta and had believed that Lori was content with her life as it was. Atlanta would be a big change. As usual, though, Devin said very little. She continued to wash Lori's hair and listen to her talk. Every now and then, she would make some kind of sound to let Lori know that she was listening.

Devin knew that she was someone the women could bounce their ideas and problems off of. Everyone felt comfortable talking to her because she never interrupted or pushed her opinions. They usually solved whatever the matter was after talking aloud to her about it. It always amazed Devin that they knew the answer to the problems they were having but needed to talk things over with someone before making any decisions.

The door to the shop opened and Helen walked in, calling out "Hello!" Before Devin or Lori could say anything, Helen started telling them how bad her day had been.

"My head is hurting, and I really need this down time. Somebody at work is playing games with me. When I find out who it is, there is going to be hell to pay."

Lori said, "I feel sorry for that person right now." The three of them laughed.

Devin asked Helen, "Is there anything new going on with you, honey?"

"No," replied Helen, "just the same old thing. The people at my job are going to drive me insane. It is hard working in corporate America. It is so male-dominated, and they just wait on you to mess up so they can swoop in."

"Well, Lori has something going on," said Devin.

"Do not keep me in the dark," said Helen. "What is it?"

Lori repeated what she had said about moving to Atlanta.

Helen said, "Girlfriend, we have really got to talk about this."

Before she could say anything else, Christine walked in all excited. "Hey, ladies, you all should have been with me! This young thing was so fine! My toes curl just thinking about him. He put the work on me, and I gave as well as I got." She was going on about what a fine man he was, and how he made her feel ten years younger.

Devin finally said, "Christine, maybe he made you feel ten years younger because *he* was ten years younger." They all laughed.

Christine said, "You old hags are just jealous. If you'd been in my shoes last night, you would feel like you were riding on cloud nine. You can take *that* to the bank." Then she took a deep breath and said, "What's going on?"

Lori told her, "We were in the middle of a conversation, and you burst through the door and interrupted our train of thought."

Everyone laughed, and Christine said, "You gals do not have anything exciting going on. I came to liven up the house. So what's happening?"

Lori repeated her story about wanting to move. Christine was surprised and said, "I'm so glad to learn that you have some adventure still left in you, girl. You are still a good-looking woman with years of fun ahead of you. Go for it, girl!"

"Don't listen to Christine," said Helen. "You know all Christine thinks about is men, sex, and fun."

"Is there anything else?" asked Christine, "Girl, please. Life is too short. I am going to enjoy mine. My husband has been dead for a year now. What am I supposed to do? I'm going to live and let live."

For a time, they'd all been worried about Christine because she had just given up. Now, she was actually dating and enjoying life again. She had no children and plenty of money. They all thought girlfriend had it made and were happy for her. She was also going through a stay-young phase, and no one took her seriously about important matters.

Nevertheless, they all looked forward to her stories about her new young lovers. They didn't believe all of her stories, but they were fun to listen to, and maybe some of them wished they were with those young men instead of her. However, Christine's goal was to make Yvonne uncomfortable with all of her young-guy sex talk. All the women knew that Christine got a kick out of annoying Yvonne.

Helen was younger than Christine, but she acted much older than her age. She was on her second marriage, and it was a disaster. She was holding on because to leave would mean that she had to admit to another failed marriage. They all felt that she was being abused, but they did not know for sure.

Helen was a very pretty woman. She had creamy vanilla-looking skin, not a flaw on her face, beautiful legs, and a great body. However, for some reason, she did not realize how pretty she was. She had very little confidence in herself as a woman. She dressed down and made herself look older than she was. All of the ladies thought it was a shame for her to hide all of her beauty with old dowdy clothes and a hairdo that was right out of a movie from the forties.

The subject for the day was now chosen—Lori leaving town. Yvonne and Brandi had not yet arrived. However, the conversation was hot. It would get hotter when the other two joined in.

Helen wanted to know why Lori would leave when she had not yet divorced her husband. "Lori, you should be trying to get back with your husband, not leaving town." She knew that God did not approve of divorce, and Lori should have been trying to get her marriage of forty years on track. "If you quit your job and leave, you will have to start all over," Helen went on. "It will not be easy for you at this stage of your life. What about all of your friends, children, and grandchildren? Surely you will miss all of them."

Before Lori could answer, Christine jumped in with her advice. "What is wrong with you, Helen? Age has nothing to do with her moving. She has still got it, honey. It could be an exciting time for her. All of those rich, good-looking men in Atlanta, ooh! It makes me want to move just thinking about it."

Everyone laughed. It was just like Christine to bring everything back to men.

Finally, Yvonne and Brandi arrived. Yvonne seemed a little down. Brandi was her usual cool self. Nothing seemed to bother that young thing. Lori really liked Brandi, and she believed that Brandi liked her more than she liked the others.

After Yvonne and Brandi had been brought up-to-date on the topic of the evening, Yvonne said, "Lori, you are just going through a midlife crisis, and you do not need to make any hasty decisions."

Helen agreed with this analysis of the situation. Christine, however, thought they were both full of it. She really believed that Helen just needed a good man to work her over—and Yvonne needed one too. In her opinion, they were both love-starved and living with the wrong men. In Christine's opinion, that would make anyone negative. *Both of them need a life*, Christine thought to herself.

Brandi quietly listened as the women talked. She said nothing at all. She thought it was cool of Lori to want to make this change in her life. Brandi admired the fact that after forty years of marriage, Lori had walked out on her own and got herself a place to live, a good job, and a new car. She was a sporty, sharp dresser and very smart.

Brandi could easily see Lori in Atlanta living a real good life. After all, she had family over there. She would not be alone. Brandi did not see anything wrong with Lori moving to Atlanta.

Finally, Lori looked at Brandi and said, "Okay, baby girl, what do you think?"

Brandi never looked up. She just said, "Go for it, you can do it. I would if the opportunity came up. You have to live for yourself one day, simple as that." To the other ladies, she said, "What is all the fuss about? Atlanta is only two hours away. She can see her children and grandchildren as often as she wants. She probably needs a break from all of them." Finally, turning back to Lori, she said, "I say, go for it."

The other women all laughed. "Oh, to be young and spirited again," said Devin. They really laughed now at Devin saying something. She usually just listened and nodded but rarely made a comment.

Christine started up on her new young lover again. She started telling them how he could go on and on forever. However, he was no match for her. She kept up and wore the young thing down. They were all laughing so hard, Devin almost dropped the curlers she had in her hand.

Yvonne wanted her to shut up about her new young boy toy. She kept trying to change the subject, but there was no stopping Christine, and all the others liked hearing her brag about her young boyfriends. Finally, Yvonne just gave up and listened. Though she'd never admit it, the talk was making her day.

It was nearly midnight before they were all through. Each one left, promising to see the others next Thursday.

CHAPTER 2

Another Thursday night, and the shop was quiet. Everyone was there except Helen. It was not like her to not call or be there. Christine, Yvonne, Brandi, and Lori all sat around quietly with their minds on Helen.

Christine finally spoke up and said, "I wonder what happened to Helen. She has not missed a Thursday in two years."

They all knew Helen was having problems with her husband. He could be awfully mean, they thought. Just little things Helen had said made them think he could be abusive.

Finally, Devin said, "I hope that fool did not hurt her."

All of them said amen to that.

Nobody was in a mood for talking. It was the first time in a long time that all was quiet in the beauty shop. You could actually hear the humming of the hair driers. Everyone was in deep thought. They all knew something was very wrong for Helen to not show up or call and cancel. It would not have been the first time her husband had caused her pain. She denied it, but they all knew in their hearts that he was abusive to her.

Yvonne went home from the shop and tried to relax. She had her usual Coke and bourbon. However, tonight it did not relax her. Therefore, she had two or three more. None of the women would believe that she drank. She only did it to relax her mind when she was overwhelmed.

Tonight she felt very uneasy, as if something was happening that would change all of them. Yvonne did not like change at all. It was so unlike Helen to not show up or call, and Yvonne was worried about her friend. She fixed herself another drink. As long as she did not get drunk, it is not a sin. It was just the way she tried to relax. She knew that something bad had kept Helen from the shop, and that really worried her.

Yvonne fixed another drink and went to bed. As her eyes closed, her last thought was of Helen. Friday morning, as soon as she got up, she called to see if Devin had heard from Helen. When Devin said she had called the power company and Helen was not there, Yvonne got a bad feeling about the situation. She said a silent prayer for Helen.

Lori also called Devin that morning. She had been wanting to call Helen herself but didn't have the phone number. It dawned on her that she never saw or talked to Helen except for Thursday at the beauty shop. She never saw any of the women except at Devin's salon. Lori had no way of contacting any of them, and they had all been friends now for nearly four years. Helen and the other girls had become so important to her.

As she poured herself another cup of coffee and looked out her kitchen window, Lori began to say a prayer for Helen's safety. She also made herself a promise that she would have more contact with her friends, get their phone numbers, and give them hers. The only one who had everyone's number was Devin. If Devin had not heard from Helen, then something was wrong. Lori could feel it in her bones. She shivered as a cold chill passed over her body.

Christine was glad that Friday was finally here. She crawled out of bed and stumbled into the bathroom. She wondered why she was in such a foul mood. Being with the gang at the beauty shop had been no fun last night. Damn Helen, why wouldn't she call and let somebody know she was not coming?

Chris was upset because she'd had a hot story to tell and she never got the chance to say anything. She started running her bathwater. As she stepped into the tub, again her thoughts went to Helen. *Where in the hell was she last night?* Then she thought how little she really knew about any of her salon friends. She had never been outside of Devin's little shop with any of them. She wondered what those women were like in the outside world. As she sank into the hot water, she prayed that Helen was safe and doing well.

Helen woke up Friday morning feeling tired. She had not rested well. She got out of bed and went into the bathroom. She tried to avoid the mirror so she would not see how bruised her face was. She knew the girls were probably worried about her. However, she did not want them to see her looking like this—face and arms all bruised, lip swollen. She was so ashamed. She was at her sister's house. She could not understand what had happened to her or why.

On Wednesday night, after working twelve long hours, she had taken her bath and gone to bed. David, her husband, was not home. She had tried to stay awake but was so tired that she fell asleep. She awoke startled, feeling hands all over her body. David had come in and was kissing on her. She tried to wake up and respond to him, but she was so tired. She kept falling back to sleep.

He got upset and started beating her about her face and head with his fists. She tried to get out of bed, but he had her pinned down. She could smell alcohol on his breath. The smell and the weight of his body were suffocating her. The pain in her face and head was unbearable.

"Please, David," she pleaded, "stop before you hurt me bad." Repeatedly she pleaded with him to stop hitting her. She was also groggy from sleep, but she finally got away from him and ran out of the room. She saw her car keys and purse on the table. She grabbed them and ran out to her car. She felt blood running down her face. She was shaking so bad she could hardly start the car.

In the rearview mirror of her car, she saw David coming out of the house. She was so afraid. She locked the doors to the car and hurried to get it started. Just as he approached the car, she got it in drive and sped away. She could hear him cursing and calling her names as she drove away from the house as fast as she could. He was calling her vile names and cursing loudly. He was acting like a wild man. She kept wondering why he did this to her.

Then she realized that she was only in her nightgown. No coat, no shoes on her feet. She could feel the tears rolling down her face. She did not know where she was going or who would help her. She didn't want her mom and dad to see her like this. It would kill them to know she was beaten. She could not bring this problem to them.

Helen and her sister were very close. Lillie was the only one she could turn to. She got on the freeway and headed to her sister's house.

As she was driving down the freeway, she thought, *Tomorrow is Thursday, and I will miss my appointment at the beauty shop.* Then she laughed. Here she was driving down the freeway bruised and bleeding, in a nightgown, and her first thought was about her beauty appointment. She felt like she was going insane. Her whole world was turned upside down.

Helen called off from work and stayed in bed as she tried to figure out what to do next. This was not the first time he had hurt her, and she knew it would not be the last. She thought of the girls at the shop, but she was too ashamed to go or call. She stayed in bed crying and wishing she could talk to them. She needed to get her clothes. In the meantime, it was a good thing she and her sister could wear the same size.

Lillie had been so angry when she saw Helen's face. "Why do you continue to put up with David?"

Helen said nothing. Lillie wanted to call the police, but Helen said no. She did not want the police involved. She was too ashamed of what had happened to tell strangers about it. She needed time to think and decide what she was going to do. One thing she knew for sure: she was not going back into the life she had been living. She had to figure out what she wanted to do.

CHAPTER 3

Friday night, Christine had a date with a new young hunk. He was in his early twenties and very good looking. She had really been looking forward to this evening. She was feeling the need to be touched, and she meant to get touched. She took a long leisurely bath with her best bath oil. Her hair was looking very good. She had bought a cute but very sexy dress, and she would be out for fun tonight. She did not want to think of anything but getting her groove on.

Now, she was dressed and waiting for her date. The music was on. Marvin Gaye's "Sexual Healing" was playing. The drinks were ready; it was almost time for her date to arrive. Marvin's voice was really getting her in the mood. She began to hum along.

The doorbell rang. *It's on now*, she thought as she took one last look in the mirror at herself. She opened the door and looked into the brownest eyes she had ever seen. She smiled and said, "Hi, handsome. I been waiting on you all my life." She gave him her biggest smile as she led him into the room.

Wait until I tell the girls about this night. Helen popped into Christine's mind, but she pushed the thought into the back. She was going to teach this young thing something tonight. Everything and everyone else would have to wait. She smiled and looked into those gorgeous brown eyes and asked him what he wanted to drink.

He said, "Whatever you got, honey."

"Then scotch it is," said Christine. "Just make yourself at home." She thought, *I have struck gold tonight*.

They began to drink one drink after another. Christine tried conversation. It was no use. They had nothing in common. The only thing left was bed. Finally, they went into the bedroom.

The next morning, Christine woke up with a headache. *Too many drinks last night. What an awful night,* she thought. She rolled over in bed and realized that the young thing was still there. She jumped up and ran into the bathroom. She did not want him to wake up and see her before she had a chance to get herself together.

She looked into the mirror and saw that she was showing signs of age. She'd made him keep the lights off last night. Nevertheless, she knew that he felt all the extra layers on her body. His passion was disappointing as he drank more and more. She felt that he was drinking in order to deal with being with her. He was a big disappointment to her. Now she just wanted him gone. She was so ashamed of herself.

Why did she continue to put herself through this kind of thing? She ran her bath water. Christine just wanted him to get the hell out of her house. She had hoped he would be gone when she got out of the tub, but he was still snoring loudly. He was reeking of alcohol when she woke him and told him he had to leave. She went into another room and stayed until she heard the door close. She began to cry, and she could feel a depression coming on.

She started doing her secret thing to make her feel better: she lit a blunt and inhaled deeply. As the warm feeling came over her, she thought about what she would tell the gang about last night. The higher she got, the better everything started to look to her. She would really pump up the story for them.

Yvonne was a frustrated woman. Nothing exciting ever happened in her life. Her marriage was comfortable but dull. Her sex life was just plain boring. Her job was nothing special, but it paid well. She wished that just once, something exciting would happen to her.

She had the same old routine day in and day out. She daydreamed a lot, and she felt guilty about that. The fact that she drank every now and then made her feel guilty. She was very religious, and that is why Christine got on her nerves with all of her talk about young men and sex. How could Christine think those young men desired her? Yvonne wanted so bad to tell her to grow up and act her age. She had no morals, no morals at all.

What was so exciting about sex? She and her husband, Robert, had a date every Saturday night to have sex. It was mainly for him to relieve himself. She got nothing out of it, but it made him happy. She went along for the ride. One night after listening to Christine talk about sex and all of its pleasure, she came home and tried to snuggle with Robert, but he thought she was out of line. The truth of the matter was, she had scared him because he was not used to her being affectionate at all. Therefore, he did not know how to react to her that night. Yvonne never tried again.

Robert was trying hard to live up to Yvonne's puritanical view of that side of marriage. It was just a duty to her, and he suppressed his feelings in order not to upset her sensitive nature. Yvonne thought that she was behaving the way he wanted his Christian wife to behave. They were both miserable and did not know what to do about it.

Every Saturday night at nine p.m. exactly, he patted her on the left buttock and said, "Come on to bed." Before 9:30 p.m., it was all over until the following Saturday. Robert would get out of bed and go for a walk. Yvonne would stay in bed feeling empty and lost, but without knowing why. She'd get up, fix herself a small drink, and go to sleep.

Yvonne hated to admit it, but deep down inside she lived for Christine's conversations, even though they were disgusting to her. She told herself she was going to burn in hell for listening, but she listened anyway. Yvonne knew there was something missing in her relationship with Robert, but she didn't know what to do about it. She was frustrated, and she believed that Robert was too. Still, they never talked about it. They never discussed their feelings at all. Things remained the same, each of them acting as if life between the two of them was great.

Lori could not believe how fast the week had gone by. She'd made her decision to move to Atlanta for good, and she wanted to tell the girls. It was not an easy choice for her to make, but she wanted to see if she could conquer some of her lost dreams.

She'd always wanted to live in Atlanta, and she was going to go for it. Who knew what was waiting for her there? She really hoped Helen was okay and would be at Devin's today. She really wanted the whole gang there. She knew they would have plenty to say—especially that Christine. No telling what that woman and Brandi would say.

The hours were really flying. Almost time for her to go.

Devin had been to the beauty supply store to stock up on supplies. All the girls had called for their appointment, so she was resting now. She knew she would be working until midnight. All of the talking slowed her down, but she would not have it any other way.

I know all of these women's secrets, she thought. They all talked to her one-on-one. Sometimes they told her things when they were alone that they did not tell the group. Devin treasured every conversation. She would never repeat anything they told her in secret, and they all knew that. Devin did not need the money from her Thursday clients as much as she needed the friendships. Her husband provided for her very well. The women would be surprised if they knew just how well off she was.

She got up and started preparing for their arrival. She was anxious to hear what had happened to Helen last Thursday. They were all coming in earlier today, but it would still be late when they left. She smiled and kept getting things in order.

At 1:00 p.m., the door to the shop opened, and Christine, Yvonne, and Lori walked in, laughing together. Christine had already started talking about her new young stud. Lori and Christine were laughing, and Yvonne was frowning as usual. All of the sex talk was getting on her nerves. She did not understand how Lori could laugh so hard about it at her age.

"Devin, is Helen coming today?" Lori asked.

"Yes, she is coming, and so is Brandi," said Devin.

"Oh Lord," said Christine, "the conversation will really be hot if Brandi is going to be here."

They all laughed. Brandi was a stripper—or exotic dancer, as she liked to called herself. Brandi took pride in enlightening everyone on her profession, as she considered herself an expert on men.

Brandi was young, wild, and good looking. She came from a good family. Her parents had six children, and she was the youngest and different from all the others. She went to college but left after something happened to her. She became pregnant and had a beautiful son. Got religion and then reverted to dancing. She was a complicated person but a loving and dedicated mother to her son.

Brandi was something else—she had plans to change her life. Brandi did not intend to dance all of her life. She had big dreams for herself, and one day she was going to tell these women her dreams. She also had no doubt that she would make all of her dreams come true. She knew that life had more to offer her, and she was going to get it.

Helen opened the door and walked in. She was wearing shades. All of the women started talking at her at once.

Christine asked, "Where the hell were you last week, girl? I had things to talk about."

Lori asked her, "What's with the shades? Don't tell me you're going Hollywood on us."

Everyone laughed but Helen. She slowly removed the shades, and everyone became quiet. Her face was bruised and her eyes were swollen. They all gathered around and began hugging her. No one asked any questions. In her own time, she would talk to them. At the moment, they just wanted to let her know they cared and were there for her.

However, when Brandi finally arrived, she took one look at Helen and started asking the questions that were on everyone's mind.

"Brandi, leave her alone," Lori cautioned. "She will tell us when she's ready."

But Helen was ready now. As she told the whole story, she was crying very hard.

Brandi looked at her and said, "Dump him and find you someone else. It's just that simple—just do it. I would have killed him if that had been me. I promised myself that no man would ever beat up on me again in this lifetime."

The hatred and venom in her voice startled the other women. They had never heard Brandi sound like that. The look on her face told the story behind the words. It was at that moment they all realized that Brandi had been through some horrible ordeals in her young life. That would explain many of the things Brandi would say and do. They all felt that she needed help. Each one of the women in her own heart knew she had to help her. However, Helen needed them right now.

The conversation was now on. Yvonne told Brandi, "It is not a simple matter, because God does not approve of divorce. Helen has to do everything in her power to keep the marriage together." To Helen, Yvonne said, "You need to talk with your minister or a Christian counselor."

Christine spoke up and said, "Yvonne, you are full of bull. David hurt her; he is the one who needs counseling."

"I will drink to that," said Devin.

Lori was very quiet as she listened to them go back and forth about what Helen should do. She was thinking of her situation—how long it had taken her to go out on her own. She felt empathy for Helen. It had taken her almost forty years to break free. She had lived with an alcoholic for all forty years. She had suffered abuse both mentally and physically. She could not even today tell anyone why it took her so long to break free. She knew what Helen was feeling, and she knew how hard it was to admit your life was a lie and a failure.

Lori remembered when she finally realized that she could no longer live her life that way. It was as if something snapped inside of her, and she had to break free or die. When she walked out, it felt as if layers of depression and fear were falling off her. It was as if she was being reborn.

Lori knew what abuse did to a woman. She also knew it was hard to break from an abusive situation and that only Helen could make the decision to recapture her life. Her heart went out to Helen, but she remained silent through most of the conversation. Lori knew that Helen probably felt that what was happening to her was her fault and she was doing something wrong to make David treat her the way he did. Lori thought to herself, *Brandi, you are not the only one who has been in a dark cave with a man and had to fight your way out.*

"What do you want to do, Helen?" Lori asked.

Helen looked at Lori and started crying. It was painful for her to talk about how she felt. She finally said, "This is my second marriage, and I feel like a failure. Why can't I get a man who will love and cherish me? What am I doing wrong? Another divorce, living alone—I am dreading that. David called me saying that he's sorry, it won't happen again, but I know it will. It always does. I really wish that I could believe him, but I know that I can't trust him. I have to face that each time, it gets worse. He has never beaten me this way before. I'm afraid that the next time he will kill me. I am afraid of him. He can be so loving one minute, and the next minute he is a very different person. There is a very dark side of him, and I am afraid of that side."

"Do whatever your heart is telling you to do," said Lori. "Listen to that inner voice that is your spirit and trust what it is telling you. Only you can decide what you need to do."

Helen said, "It is telling me to get out of this before he kills me. He is going to kill me if I do not stay away from him. He becomes violent toward me for any little reason. He makes up reasons to get angry with me. I know if I stay with him, he will kill me one day. I am so afraid of him."

"There—you have your answer," said Lori. "That is how I got my answer: by listening to my inner voice, my spirit, and following it. Trust your heart, and don't be afraid. You are much stronger than you think, and you do not need a man who beats you in your life. The decision is yours to make. We will support you in whatever decision you make and any way we can. You can count on us to be there for you."

Brandi was listening and thinking to herself about all the times her baby's father had beaten her, and the man she finally married. She took all kinds of abuse from both of them. Now she did not give a damn about any man. All she wanted was what she could get from them. God help the one who tried to hit her again. She was divorced, and she was going to stay that way.

In the end, Brandi thought, *they all treat you like dirt.* She told Helen, "Leave the fool and get all you can in the process. Walk out and do not look back. That is what I did. I cannot remember what they look like now—my husband or my son's father. They were both bastards."

Devin never commented. Every now and then, she would nod her head or say something like, "I know what you mean." She was an Oprah fan. Watched her TV show every day. Therefore, she knew that Helen probably blamed herself for her troubled marriage, and she knew that the Oprah show had given good advice to women on abuse and self-esteem. She thought, *Helen needs Oprah and Dr. Phil.*

Lori knew that they could not solve this today. Only Helen could decide what she should do. In an attempt to lighten the conversation, Lori told them all about her decision to move to Atlanta.

Brandi spoke up and said, "You are one cool lady, and you love excitement, don't you?"

"What are you talking about, Brandi?" asked Lori.

"Well, leaving your husband after nearly forty years of marriage. Moving into that fabulous townhouse. Going back to work after not working for years. You are something else," Brandi told her.

Everyone laughed. Brandi always made everything seem so simple. Just like Nike, her motto was, "Just do it."

Yvonne was shocked. "Why in heaven's name would you give up all you have to move to Atlanta at your age?"

Lori wanted to slap her face, just shake her very hard. Yvonne was such an old stick-in-the-mud for a young woman.

Lori looked at Yvonne and quietly asked, "Do you ever dream? Is there anything special in life that you would like to do if you had the chance? Do you ever wish sometime that you could start over fresh? Invent something or say something that was so profound that it would change the world? Write a book. Parachute out of a plane. Travel around the world. I still dream, and I have dreams that I would like to accomplish before I leave this world. I have not given up on life, and I know that it is not over for me. Not yet."

She continued, "I have raised my six children, lived in a marriage for forty years that was doomed from the start, said yes to everybody for everything they wanted me to do—now I feel that I can say yes to things that *I* want to do. I can now climb some of the mountains that seemed so out of reach to me. So now, I am saying yes to me. I will not wake up ten years from now decrepit with regrets for not trying to do some of the things that I wanted to do."

"You go, girl," said Brandi. "I'll come and visit you."

Lori laughed and said, "You and me, Brandi, roommates."

They all laughed—except Yvonne.

They were all just about ready to leave when Brandi said, "Chris, what did you have to tell us?"

Chris laughed and started to tell them about her young stud—how he could not get enough of her and how good he was in the sack. Yvonne left, totally disgusted with all of them. Finally, they all said good night. Devin stood at the door and called out to them, "Until next week, ladies. Be safe."

CHAPTER 4

Yvonne was upset when she got home. Helen was not getting good advice from the others. She was surprised at Lori, and Chris was a disgrace. Lori was clearly going through a midlife crisis, and Yvonne prayed she would come to her senses. Brandi was a lost cause—she was a stripper, after all, and Yvonne thought she had no morals at all.

I will just stop going on Thursdays, Yvonne told herself. She ran herself a bath, and as she sank slowly into the water, she felt herself becoming aroused. She could hear Chris describing all of those things that young boy did to her. Yvonne put her hands on her body in a way she had never done before. It felt good.

She panicked. *What am I doing? This is a sin!* She began to pray for forgiveness. Yvonne was so confused. The good feeling would not go away; she had to quiet her body, and she did. She blamed Chris and promised herself she would not go back to the shop on Thursdays. She dried herself off and went to bed. However, she got no rest. The feelings came back. Yvonne tossed and turned until she finally went to sleep.

Just before she closed her eyes, she looked at the clock and wondered why Robert was so late getting home. He was coming home later and later every night. Yvonne felt he was working too hard. She knew that owning his own business meant a lot to him. The business was doing well, and he made good money. But there was no reason for him to work so hard and so long. Yvonne made a mental note to talk with him about it.

They only came together on Saturday nights, and now he was working late on Saturdays too. She'd be asleep when he got home, but she felt that she must talk to him. She didn't have the courage to tell him that she needed and wanted him home with her.

Brandi left the shop and went straight to work. She wanted so bad to tell Yvonne that her husband was one of the club's best clients. Brandi worked at the Shangri-La, a club for men. She was an exotic dancer there. She knew that men would part with their money for a good fantasy.

The women at the salon could talk about her all they wanted. She was the one with the new car, a growing bank account, and a nice place to live. Her son was in private school and not on welfare. No man was beating her, telling her what to do, or mistreating her son. No, she was happy and doing just fine just as she was.

Man, she realized, *I forgot to stop and buy myself a bottle of scotch.* She always needed a drink before she could get up there on stage and perform. The liquor helped her be free and dance the way she knew the men wanted. Brandi was not in love with this kind of work, but it paid her the money that allowed her and her son to live well. She needed the alcohol to give her the courage to strip in front of all those men night after night. There was no way she could do it sober.

The looser she was, the more money flew out of their pockets. She drank so she could forget what she was doing and where she was. Yvonne's husband was her best customer, and she knew he would be there. He always wanted a private performance, and she was the only one he wanted to dance for him. Poor Yvonne. She was such a nerd. She needed to turn into a whore in the bedroom before her man went broke coming to the club all the time.

Oh well! It's show time, and after all, it is not my business whose husband comes into the club. I am not sending for him. He comes of his own free will. That is how she saw it. Brandi had no guilt feelings about dancing for Yvonne's husband. Better her than some of the other women who would take him home, and then Yvonne would really lose out. *I am helping Yvonne keep her man.* That was how Brandi justified dancing for him. She was actually doing Yvonne a favor.

Christine went home and fixed herself a scotch and water, lit a blunt, and started to get high. She was taking stock of herself. Here she was, an attractive woman, plenty of money, nice home, three cars. She had her own business that was doing very well. Overall, she had it going on.

But she had no real love in her life. She had never wanted children and never had any. She knew she was getting too old for barhopping and clubs. However, older men bored her. She liked young men. She felt young and alive with them.

She knew that a lot of them were with her because she was paying for everything and letting them use her cars and her. She wished that just one of them wanted her for herself. Christine was beginning to realize that she was not happy with these young men. She was putting on a little weight, and her hair was turning gray. Devin had started to put a rinse in it. Age was creeping up on her fast, but she intended to fight it all the way.

She poured herself another drink, looked at her empty bed, and left the room. She was going to sleep on the sofa in the den with the television for company. Christine hated being alone. The blunt and alcohol helped her cope on the nights she did not have a partner to stay with her. She thought Helen would soon see what it was like to be alone. Sometimes a piece of a man is better than no man. Nevertheless, who wants to be mistreated all the time?

Lori was laughing on the way home about how easily Christine could get to Yvonne. She knew that Helen would do what was best. No matter what the decision, Lori would support her friend. As for herself, she had made up her mind. She was resigning her job and getting started on her plans to move.

Helen was living what Lori had gotten out of. She and her husband had married very young. He was twenty and she was sixteen. He was the love of her life. The love of her life turned into a disaster so fast it scared her.

He became a heavy drinker and womanizer. He hit her a few times but never beat her like Helen's husband had. He was psychologically abusive to her. He kept her down and, for a long time, afraid of life. After years and years of this kind of treatment, she finally broke away. She was doing just fine, and Helen would be fine. Helen would learn that he was a coward, and the only person he could conquer was his wife—and now that she was gone, he would be scared and never bother her again. Lori thought to herself, *One day, I will tell Helen my story.* However, for now, she was going to pray for Helen to make wise decisions about her life.

Brandi was finally at the club. She had to decide which costume to wear. Robert liked the red outfit, and she needed money. She dressed and looked in the mirror. She knew that she looked sexy. *Money honey* was the look she had. She shook her butt and entered the main club room.

She smiled as the men hollered for her. She stopped at the bar for a couple of drinks, and then she was ready for show time.

She stepped onto the stage and went into her act. The place was going wild and the money was coming out of the men's pockets, and that was all Brandi wanted.

She spotted Robert as he walked into the club, so she really turned it on. As he stood watching her, she could see the desire in his eyes, and she knew that he would pay well tonight. He never touched her. He just wanted her alone performing only for him, and he would call her Yvonne as she danced. She didn't get it, nor did she care as long as he paid. Whatever was happening with him and Yvonne was their business, not hers.

Devin hated to see Lori leave. She was a smart, attractive woman, and Devin found her very interesting. She read all kinds of books and loved people and music, but there was a sadness about her that Devin could not figure out. Devin herself was married. She and her husband were as much in love today as they were when they first met. They loved spending time together.

Devin just wished that her husband would take better care of his health. She was forever trying to get him to exercise more. He owned his own cleaning service. The company employed over three hundred people and had two offices. Therefore, life was very good to them. They only had one son, and he was a doctor in New York. They were both very proud of him. He was still single and did not seem ready to settle down with a family at this time in his life. She had quit her job after the business became profitable and decided to go to cosmetology school and get her beauty-shop license.

Devin just wanted to operate a small salon out of her house. Therefore, she had converted her basement into a salon. She had her select few clients and was happy. She just wanted to keep this group of women together. One for all and all for one. In her mind, this was the perfect setting.

One day, she thought, *I am going to write a book, and I will be famous.* No one knew that Devin's dream was to become a best-selling author. Listening to Lori talk about dreams had really brought it back home to her.

Even as a young girl, she would dream about being a famous author. *I can see me now*, she thought, *on the Oprah show. My book will be on Oprah's Book Club list.* She started smiling and daydreaming. She could see herself at the Academy Awards because her book was made into a movie and it was up for best picture and it won. Then Oprah herself would invite her to be on the Oprah show along with the actors who starred in the movie. Devin took the handle of the broom, stood in front of the mirror, and practiced her acceptance speech. She bowed to the imaginary audience. She had this conversation with Oprah in her mind, talking about their yachts and homes in California.

You are so right to dream, Lori, for I am dreaming with you, thought Devin. Lori was right—Yvonne needed to learn how to dream. Maybe she would lighten up some.

Helen was still with her sister, and even though the idea of divorce was distasteful to her, she knew she had no choice. She saw a lawyer and started the divorce proceedings. Now she needed a place to live.

Helen thought about Lori and the condominium she lived in. It was beautiful, and Lori seemed to have been so happy living there. She called the complex office, and they approved her for a condominium that same day. Getting her things out of the house would be her next challenge.

Helen hired movers, and on a day when David had to go out of town on business, Helen moved her things out of the house and into her new home. That night, for the first time in weeks, she had a peaceful sleep. Everything she had brought into the marriage she took out of the house. She did not have very much to move. Helen bought all new furniture for her new place. That was the way she wanted it. Everything fresh and new.

Helen spent the rest of the week getting her place in order. By the weekend, it looked as if she had always lived there. The only thing left was the divorce becoming final. She could feel her spirit returning, and she knew that she was connecting to it. Her confidence was soaring.

She was beginning to think about changing her career. She wanted to go into some kind of business. She was going to be on the lookout for something interesting to invest in. Her own company. That would be something.

CHAPTER 5

A strange thing happened to Christine. She met the man of her dreams, and he was her age. He was a retired widower, and he had moved into the house next door to her. He had lived there for quite a while before she met him. He was average looking, but he had a warm smile.

They met by accident. Christine was high and drove her car onto his lawn and flowerbeds. To make matters worse, she passed out in the car. He came out of his house and was upset about his yard but very concerned for her. He knew that she lived next door, for he had seen her going in and out of her house.

He did not call the police. He removed her from the car and carried her into his house. He knew that she was not hurt, just drunk. He laid her on the sofa and covered her with a blanket. He was going to let her sleep it off.

He removed the car from his yard and put it in her driveway. The damage to the car was minor, and the yard could be fixed. He walked back into his den and sat in a chair across from the sofa, watching this attractive woman sleeping. He wondered what was going on in her life for her to be drunk at one o'clock in the afternoon on a beautiful Saturday like this.

As Christine started to come out of her alcohol-induced sleep, she realized she did not recognize the room she was in. As her eyes began to focus, she saw a man sitting and looking at her. *Who is he and how in hell did I get here?* She wondered. She closed her eyes and pretended to be sleeping while she tried to remember who he was and how she got there.

He knew she was not asleep, so he started talking to her. "Are you feeling better? Does anywhere hurt you?"

Why is he asking me do I hurt? Christine asked herself. *What is wrong with him and why would I be hurting?*

"I'm your next-door neighbor, Frank Martin," he said. "You had a small accident. You drove your car into my yard and passed out."

She kept her eyes closed. She just wanted to disappear. She was so embarrassed.

Frank guessed how she was feeling, and he started trying to put her at ease. "This happens to the best of us. Your car is not bad, and the yard is fixable." He started laughing. "You have changed the design of the yard."

He was laughing very hard, so she opened her eyes, and they started laughing together. They spent the rest of the day together and had been seeing each other on a regular basis since that awful day she drove into his yard.

At 3 p.m. Thursday, all the women were at Devin's. Lori noticed that Helen seemed to be extremely happy, and she commented on it. Helen laughed and said, "I have never felt better in my life. I feel as if I have been released from prison."

She looked good. She had changed her style of dressing, and she seemed to have confidence in herself.

"What do you mean about the prison thing?" asked Christine.

"I have been so afraid, Chris, of being alone and not having a man in my life, until I lost myself trying to hold on to what I did not really have. I became a prisoner of all my own fears. I let that man bully me and then make me feel that I was responsible for his bad conduct. I am no longer afraid of him. I am free for the first time in years."

"Look out, girls. The woman sounds like she is going through counseling," said Christine.

"That's right, I am," Helen told them. "I am really facing many things about myself. If there is ever another man in my life, fine, and if there is not, fine. I am not depending on anyone else to make me happy. I can do that myself."

"You go, girl," said Brandi. "I know what you mean. I am free to live my way. No man holds me captive. Girl, I am so glad to see you come out of your shell."

They all laughed—except Yvonne. She had promised herself that she would not come today. Nevertheless, she found herself driving to Devin's house. She was miserable and lonely. Robert was working later and later every night. Even their coming together on Saturday nights was being put on hold. Something was not right.

She just did not have the courage to talk to Robert about her feelings and fears. She could not bring herself to tell him how lonely she was. She was also afraid that he had found another woman. She was miserable, but she could not bring herself to talk to the women about it either. She could not tell anyone.

"What are you thinking about, Yvonne?" asked Lori.

Yvonne smiled and said, "Just work. I am working on a big project. So all I think about is work," she lied.

Brandi looked at her and kind of felt sorry for her. Her husband was in the club every night. Therefore, she knew that he was not spending any time with Yvonne. Brandi thought Yvonne should work on her marriage, and maybe her man would stay home.

"I have some exciting news to tell everyone," said Christine. "So I want you all to get quiet and listen to what I am about to say: *I am in love.*"

What is new about that? The women all thought. They started laughing, but Christine was not laughing, and they noticed that she had a serious look on her face.

"Truly, everyone, I am in love. I have met the man of my dreams. He is not one of these foolish young things that I have been associating with in the past. He is the real deal. His name is Frank Martin, and he lives right next door to me. He has been under my nose all of this time, and I did not know he existed. Nevertheless, I know now. He is two years older than I am. He is loving and caring. He is also a widower and has a daughter. He is going to be a grandfather soon. I cannot wait for you women to meet my man."

The others were all dumbfounded. She was blushing, and they could see that she was falling hard for this person. She told them she had not slept with him. Now they were really in shock. She described their dates as just enjoying each other's company and really getting to know one another. She was very happy about that.

Life was looking good to her. She looked so happy. Yvonne was happy for her friend, but she was feeling so bad for herself.

Christine was really changing, and it seemed this man was responsible for the change. She was losing weight. They all notice she was letting the gray in her hair come out, and it looked good. She really seemed happy. There was something beautiful about her. Her eyes glowed when she talked about Frank.

They were all so happy for her. They continued to ask Christine more and more questions about Frank, and she was very happy to answer them. Only Yvonne was quiet, and she even began to look sad. Lori could feel her pain and wished she would talk about whatever was bothering her. However, she said nothing.

Brandi also noticed how sad Yvonne seemed and felt that she was, in a way, contributing to that pain. She tried to tell herself that she was not doing anything wrong, but Yvonne was one of her friends, and yes, she felt bad about what she had been doing with Yvonne's husband. For the first time, Brandi really felt disgusted about what she did for a living. At least, it was the first time she had allowed herself to admit that she hated dancing. She really hated this work, and soon it was going to be over for her. She was working on a plan to get out of the business.

Lori told them she and her sister were renting a townhome together in Atlanta. They were going to live as bachelorettes in the big city. Lori was excited about the move and had decided that if it worked, then it worked. If it did not work out, then it did not work out. However, she would not have any regrets about not trying.

Lori said, "Ladies, I am going to throw a going-away bash before I leave, and you are all invited. I am going to have it at my house, and

I will let you know when. I want all of you to write all of your info in this book of mine. I do not intend to lose touch with any of you. I love all of you women, and you all mean so much to me."

Finally, it was time to go. They all hugged each other and said, "See you next week." Devin joined in as she closed the door after them.

Devin spent some time picking up the place, but her mind was on Yvonne. She wondered what was going on with that girl. *You can see she is just miserable. She needs to talk to us and let us try to help her.*

Yvonne got into her car and felt tears welling up in her eyes. All of the girls seemed so happy and excited about their lives—all except her. She felt hungry, so she decided to drive across town to the new Chinese restaurant and get a takeout order. She really did not like coming to this side of town by herself, and the restaurant was across the street from that club Shangri-La that Brandi worked at. All those men would be hanging around. She felt that the area was sleazy around the club. She really hated it, but here she was.

She drove to the restaurant and felt lucky to find a parking place right in front of the door. She hurried in and placed her order. It did not take long, and she was ready to be on her way. As she came out of the door of the restaurant, she looked across the street and saw her husband, Robert. She started to call out to him, but she froze as he placed his hand on the door of the club and went in. She felt herself go numb. She thought she was going to faint. Why was he going in there?

She made it to her car, but she could not make herself start the engine. She just sat there. She got out of the car and ran across the street to the club. She stood frozen at the door. Finally, she got the nerve to go in. It was dark and smoky. She could barely see her way around. All the women looked as if they were working in the club. Most of them were half-naked. A man tried to stop her, but she hurried away from him.

She tried to spot Robert, and finally she saw him go into a room and the door close. She thought she was going to be sick. She hurried back to her car. Finally, she turned the key in the ignition, and the car took her home. It never occurred to her to go and see what he was doing in the room. She just wanted out of there. It seemed as if she was in slow motion.

She was no longer hungry, so she put the food in the refrigerator. Took her bath. Poured herself a drink. She did everything but think. At three a.m., Robert finally came home. She pretended to be asleep. When he got into bed, he stayed as far away from her as he could. She thought he was going to fall out of the bed; he was so close to the edge. Far, far away from her.

She could feel the pain building up in her chest and consuming her entire body. He finally started snoring. She looked at the ceiling the rest of the night, finally falling asleep at daybreak. When she opened her eyes, again Robert was gone.

She called her job and said she was taking time off, for she had an emergency. She got back in bed, and a scream rose from the pit of her stomach up into her throat. She heard the sound, and it was some time before she realized she was the one screaming. She now knew why Brandi was looking at her with pity in her eyes. She wondered if Brandi knew that Robert was her husband. Now she felt humiliated. She got out of bed and fixed herself a drink. A strong drink. She took the bottle of scotch and got back into bed.

When Brandi left the girls, she went straight to work. She had decided to let Robert know that he needed to go home and not spend so much time at the club. She was really feeling sorry for Yvonne and bad about her part with Robert. Sure enough, when Robert came in, he asked her to privately dance for him. She talked to him. She told him that he needed to stay out of the club. Brandi told Robert, "You are a good person, and you have a wife. You need to spend time with her. I know that you love her, because the whole time I am dancing for you, you are calling her name."

He said he loved his wife, but she just would not or could not be what he wanted in a woman. He believed that Yvonne did not care about the intimate part of their life and was happy with things the way they were. Somehow, Brandi did not think so. However, she felt better. She had tried. Now she was through with it.

After all, she had a child to support, and she was throwing away her income by sending him away. She decided that she was not dancing for him anymore and she told him so. Still, he did not leave the club. He just went and sat at the bar the rest of the evening watching all the other girls dance.

Yvonne stayed in bed and drank all day. Her phone was ringing, but she did not answer. She thought she heard the doorbell, but she did not move to see if anyone was there. She had decided that if Robert did not come home tonight, she was going to see if he was at that club. She continued to drink until she passed out.

Robert came home around midnight. He smelled alcohol the minute he came into the bedroom. One bottle was empty on the floor, and another open bottle was half-full on the nightstand. Spilled alcohol was on the carpet, and Yvonne was naked, passed out on the bed. He tried to wake her but he could not.

He could not believe what he was seeing. He wondered what in the hell had happened to cause her to do something like this. She smelled awful when he picked her up and carried her to the bathroom. He turned the shower on cold and stood her under the water. The shock of the cold water hitting her body started to sober her up some. She tried to get out, but he held her there.

Finally, he took her out, dried her off, and put a robe on her. He laid her back on the bed while he made a pot of strong coffee. He forced coffee into her mouth. She became sick and stumbled into the bathroom. She just wanted to die, she was so sick.

Yvonne could not remember why she had drunk so much—her mind was blank. She was praying for death, she felt so bad. Finally, she fell asleep. Robert sat in a chair after he changed his clothes and watched her sleep. She looked so vulnerable lying there. *What in hell caused this?* He wondered.

He was also thinking about his conversation with Brandi and wondered what had brought that on. Why would she care about him and his wife? She didn't know his wife, so why did she care? Both women confused him with their actions. *When Yvonne wakes up,* he thought, *she had better have a good explanation.*

Christine had not been this happy with a man since her husband died. Frank was a perfect gentleman. They went out to eat and took long walks together. They laughed at nothing and just enjoyed being in each other's company. Christine was so comfortable with him there was no need for drugs and alcohol in her life.

Frank's daughter lived in New York with her husband. She was expecting her first child in the fall. Frank was looking forward to becoming a grandfather. Christine knew that Frank liked her for herself and that he had a lot of respect for her opinions and comments. Christine had fallen in love in with Frank. She prayed he was in love with her.

Because of the healthy way Christine was now living, she was losing weight and looking good. She had started letting the gray grow out in her hair because Frank thought the gray made her look sophisticated. She had to admit her mirror told her she was really looking good. The body was still good as well.

One night while they were talking, Frank unexpectedly said, "I love you, Christine, will you marry me?"

It caught her off guard, but she fell into his arms and they kissed.

He said, "Does this mean you will marry me?"

She said yes. She could not wait to tell the girls that she was going to get married. Lori would have to come back from Atlanta and be with her on the day of her wedding.

They had decided to have a private ceremony after the birth of his grandchild so his daughter could be there. Christine had met her and they had hit it off from the first moment. Christine and Frank were going to have a big reception for all of their friends. The girls from the salon would all be invited to the wedding. She made that clear to Frank, and it was fine with him.

Frank had started Christine attending church, and her whole outlook on life had changed for the better. She intended to get closer to Brandi, Yvonne, and Devin as well as Helen. Lori would be easy to get close to. She was such a people person. Brandi was the one she had hopes of influencing the most. She wanted that girl out of the dancing business and doing something constructive with her life. She had decided that she was going to help Brandi make a change. How she was going to accomplish this was another thing, and she had no idea where to start. However, she knew that she would find a way.

She would get the other women to help her on this project. She was going to pray for an answer.

Yvonne woke up and saw Robert sitting in the chair asleep. Her head still hurt from so much liquor, and her eyes felt heavy. However, her mind was functioning. She remembered what had set her off. She closed her eyes. She did not want to talk with Robert. He woke up and noticed that Yvonne was not asleep. He saw her eyes fluttering, and she was breathing heavy as if she was in pain. He called to her. She did not answer.

He said, "I know you're awake, and you better have a good reason for your behavior, if there is one."

Yvonne felt the anger and the pain rising up in her. She tried to control herself, but it was like a busted dam that could not be repaired. All of her anger and hurt just spilled out of her. Yvonne screamed at him, "I owe no excuse to you. If you can hang in a strip joint and leave me alone all the time, I can entertain myself any way I damn please. I saw you with my own eyes going into that club. I followed you into the club. I saw you go in a room and close the door. There is no telling what you were doing in that room. I owe you not one damn thing. You can go straight to hell. I was awake when you crept into this bed, trying to stay as far away from me as you could. I thought you were going to fall on the floor. Now I know why you do not sleep with me. You like strippers, immoral loose women. Not a God-fearing woman like I have tried to be."

She stunned Robert by her outburst. He could not speak, and that just made Yvonne madder by the minute. She continued to scream and rant at him. "Say something, damn you! You are the biggest phony that I know. Pretending that you want your wife all pure, and then you sneak around with whores."

Finally, he said, "I never slept with any of those women. I just watch them dance and fantasize about you. You have no interest in sex or being sexual. It does not bother you if we are not intimate, but Yvonne, I need that in my life. I need and want to be close to you. I want to express my love for you in every way that I can. But you will not allow me to love you. I need to hold you and be held by you. I need and desire you physically. So I go and pretend that you are the one dancing for me."

Yvonne could not believe her ears. He was telling her that he was pretending that she was a stripper. "Why in hell would you be doing that? I would never stand in front of all those men and take my clothes off!"

He told her he never wanted her to do that, just to be on fire for him sexually.

"I give you sex when you come to me," she said.

"Yvonne, you just do not get it, do you?" he asked her. "I need passion in my life, and you are not that way. I cannot and will not live like this any longer. I love you, and I want real intimacy with you, not submission for me to get relief. I want real desire and passion from you."

She was stunned by his outburst. She walked over to him and said, "You are wrong. I do need to have real intimacy with you. I love you. My whole body has been crying out for you. But you have been spending your time with strippers. I thought you were happy with things the way they were. Why didn't you talk to me? Why did you think I didn't want to be your wife in every way?"

"Honey," Robert replied, "the things you would say about sex. It was as if sex was dirty to you. You never responded or showed that you wanted me. I tried to turn on the lights, and you got upset. You never allowed me to see your body. It was as if you were ashamed of your body and mine. What else could I think? You come in here every week talking about your friend and how awful she is, talking about sex all the time. You said it was disgusting. I love you, and I did not want you to think I was disgusting because I had desires and wanted to act on them. I cannot live like this any longer with you, Yvonne, and I will not. I have to have that intimacy with my wife without feeling I am corrupting her or causing her to sin, and that is the way you make me feel. I do not want your duty. I want you to desire me as I desire you. I want you to love me, and I want to love you in every way."

Yvonne began to cry. "I love you, Robert, I love only you. I thought I was being the kind of wife that you wanted. I want to be the wife that you want in every way. I hope it is not too late for us. I love you so much."

All her life, she was told by her mother that good women did not carry on about sex. That good women did not really want sex, but it was their duty to their husband. Her mother had drilled that into her since she could remember.

Once her mother had caught her making out with a neighborhood boy; she was punished and told she was going to hell for allowing that boy to have his way with her. They were only kissing, and he had put his hand on her breast. Her mother carried her to church and made her confess that she was unclean before the whole congregation. She was taught that women who were sexual were evil women who would go to hell.

Robert knew that Yvonne's mother was cold as ice and had treated Yvonne badly. They held each other and cried. Robert and Yvonne spent the rest of the night talking and reacquainting themselves with each other. They saw how not communicating with one another had brought all of this misery into their lives. The next morning, they both stayed home together, spending the day getting to know each other better. It was going to be all right. They were going to work to make it all right between them.

Yvonne told him that she knew Brandi, and they were friends. Robert was surprised. Jokingly, she told him, "Maybe I will get Brandi to give me dancing lessons so I can dance for you." They both laughed.

Now he understood why Brandi had said the things she had said to him. Yvonne was her friend.

Yvonne laughed aloud at the look she knew Brandi would have on her face if she asked her for some pointers on dancing. Robert asked her what was so funny. She told him, "You just wait and see. But in the meantime, no more talking."

They both laughed. He started kissing her, and they both forgot about everything and everyone else.

They knew they still had plenty of work to do on their marriage, and they decided to go into counseling. Yvonne still had problems about sex that she had to overcome. Robert would be patient with her, and in time, she would feel free and completely alive in bed with her husband. She would no longer be ashamed to allow him to see her body. She had made great strides in that area. She wanted the lights on so she could see the pleasure in his face as they made love.

CHAPTER 6

Brandi had some plans of her own. She was getting tired of the club scene, and her son Danny was getting older and needing her more. She had never planned to dance forever. She had taken care of her money and was ready to make her move.

Brandi was an excellent seamstress and designer. Her dream was to have her own boutique and design her own fashions. She had some money, and she had been working on her own creations to use in the shop. She knew she would need investors, and this Thursday she was going to present her idea to the women and see if they would like to go in with her.

She was nervous about this, because this side of her the women had not seen. However, she was going to give it her best shot. Brandi had nerve, and when she wanted something, she went after it with all she had. This dress shop was her dream, and nothing was going to stop her from making her dream a reality.

Well, here it was Thursday, and Devin was getting ready for the women. She had not talked to any of them, so she hoped they would all be there. She had a feeling last week that there was definitely something wrong with Yvonne, when everyone else was upbeat. You could tell that Yvonne was not doing well. *Just maybe she will open up to us tonight if she shows up*, Devin thought to herself.

Devin looked at the clock and saw that it was almost time for the women to begin walking in the door. To her surprise, Brandi was the first one there. She had a poster and a briefcase with her.

Devin asked, "What in the world is all of this, Brandi?"

"You'll find out later," Brandi said. Devin noticed that Brandi was dressed differently also. She had on a businesslike pantsuit and very little makeup. She was stunning in the outfit. Devin had never seen her like this before.

One by one, the women all came in. Christine was bubbling over with news of her wedding. She was acting like a school girl in love for the first time. They were all so happy for her. Lori was telling them about the farewell party she was throwing. They were all laughing and talking, almost at the same time. Helen told them she was dating again, and she was not interested in settling down. She was having so much fun.

Yvonne spoke up and said, "Well, I have exciting things happening in my life for a change." The room became quiet as she started to talk. She told the girls all about what had happened with her and Robert. She told Brandi that she knew he had been spending time at the club, but he would not have any need to do that in the future, and they all laughed. She explained how not communicating with each other had almost destroyed their marriage.

She told Brandi, "I want you to teach me some dance moves so I can start giving him private shows."

"Now you're talking, girl," said Brandi.

Yvonne is definitely not the same person who was here last week, thought Devin. None of them had ever seen her this spunky, talkative, and happy. They were all happy for her.

Brandi said, "If you ladies can drop the sex talk for a moment, I have something that I would like to discuss with you. This is serious business."

"Well!" said Christine. "Listen at her all of a sudden, so prim and proper." Everyone laughed.

Brandi got out her poster and set it up on a table. She went to her car and got the outfits she had hanging in her car and brought them inside. She opened the briefcase, took out sheets of paper, and passed each woman one. She proceeded to tell them about her plans for a boutique.

They were all impressed—and not just that the dresses were beautiful and in excellent taste. The real surprise to them was that Brandi had designed and made them. Her plan was well written, and they could tell she had put a lot of thought into it.

"Damn, girl," Helen said, "you are so talented."

"I will amen that," said Devin.

"I'm not surprised that Brandi has lots of talent," said Lori. "I knew that there was more to you than you were showing. What can we do to help you?"

Brandi was so glad that Lori had asked. She told the girls that she was looking for investors. Christine and Lori said to count them in. Helen said, "I am going to invest money, but I want to be a working partner."

Everything else was forgotten, and they formed a company right then and there in Devin's little shop. The dream team had come together. There was no way this project was going to fail, for they were all of one mind. They all caught the vision that Brandi had presented. Lori's daughter-in-law was an attorney, and she would help set up their little company. This was going better than Brandi had dreamed.

They all decided to meet at Helen's house the next night to plan some more. Then it was back to their favorite subject of the moment—Yvonne, and her learning to dance for her husband. Brandi showed her a few moves but added that Yvonne would need an outfit to dance in, and she had just the outfit in her car. She went and got the red outfit that she knew Robert liked.

"Put this on and dance for him, and you will have him eating out of your hands. He will be your slave for life."

"I had better learn those steps too," said Christine. "After all, I am going to want to make Frank *my* slave for life."

They were all laughing and dancing; everyone was happy. Lori was thinking about her husband, and how she wished they could still be happy together. She pushed the thought out of her mind and told herself, *Soon I will be in Atlanta starting a new life. Therefore, I have lots to be happy about.*

Devin thought she saw a moment of sadness on Lori's face, but it did not last long. She thought, *One day when we are alone, I am going to ask her what is it that sometimes puts that sad look on her face.*

After Brandi left the shop, she was so excited about the plans she and the women were making. She started to the club but decided she was not working tonight. *I am not ever going back,* she realized. She went home, dismissed the sitter, curled up on the sofa with a drawing pad, and started working on more designs.

She had no formal training in design, but she had been making and sewing clothes ever since she was a little girl. She had made clothes for her dolls and all her friends' dolls. Then, in high school, she would design her own clothes and make them. At the club, she had made extra money designing costumes for all of the other dancers.

She had an order now she had to finish for some dancers in Florida. These would be the last costumes she would make. She was going to start cutting her ties with that part of her life. She continued drawing and planning how life was going to be.

Brandi was excited that Helen wanted to work full time with her as well as invest money in the business. All of the women had made her feel so smart and good about herself. She really loved them all. They were her family as far as she was concerned. She did not want to think about her real family. She did not need them, and she never talked about them.

She got up and looked at her son sleeping soundly in his bed, and she thought, *I am going to make you so proud of me.* He was such a handsome little fellow. *Little,* she thought. *He is seven years old now, and it won't be long before he will be asking me questions that I do not want to answer.* She wanted to make changes in her life that would make him proud of her when he was old enough to want to know what she did.

That was the main reason she wanted to get out of the business. She was fortunate that she had never been on drugs or sold her body to men. However, she knew that all of those things could happen to women in her profession. She knew of women who had danced with her that ended up on drugs and hooking. Brandi was determined that this would not happen to her. She had a plan for getting out of the business of dancing. She wanted her own business.

Getting a divorce and starting life over had proved to be the best thing Helen could have done. She had learned to be independent, and she found out that she was a smart person capable of taking care of herself. Helen no longer felt that she needed a man to validate her. She had taken control of her life. She was doing very well for herself.

Helen was so excited about this new venture with Brandi and the women. She felt that they would be a success, because they would not let themselves fail. They were all smart women. She also saw this as a chance to get on top. Helen's mindset since she got free from her husband was changing more and more each day. She was happy for Brandi, but she was going to make this work for her in many ways.

Helen finally went to bed with her mind running wild with ideas. It got so bad she had to get her pen and pad and put them by the bed so she could record the ideas that kept running into her head. Finally she fell asleep, dreaming of a brighter future.

Devin was amazed at what had happened right before her eyes. A business had been born in her shop. She had watched a dream turn into a reality.

The women were all so happy and excited about their lives now. Devin thought it was time for her to start working on her dream also. She got out a pad and pen and begun to write. Before she knew it, daylight was coming in through the window.

"Good morning, world, a lot of change is going on. And hello, Oprah, look out, here I come," Devin spoke into the air. She put down her pen and went upstairs to her bedroom. She opened the door and saw her husband lying half off the bed. His eyes were wide open, but he was not seeing anything in this world anymore.

Devin screamed and ran over to him. He was cold to her touch. She buried her head in his chest and sobbed her heart out. She called the paramedics. They told her he had died of a heart attack.

Devin had to get herself together. She needed to call their only son to come home. She would need his help. She could not go through this alone. Devin was so glad that she had her friends in her life. *I can count on them*, she thought.

She had become calm and accepted that her husband was gone. She was glad that he had not suffered. *I could not have stood seeing him in pain and suffering for a long period*, she thought. She and Jason had been kids together in the same neighborhood. Devin had always known that she loved him and that one day she would be his wife.

They had married right after college, and they were very much in love. They enjoyed spending time together. They knew each other so well. She knew what he was thinking and he knew her mind. They were so right for each other.

God, how she was going to miss having him here with her. Devin and Jason had talked about death and how they wanted whichever one was left behind to continue with life and be happy. Therefore, she knew that he would not want her to grieve over him but to honor his life by continuing with hers.

She was going to call the girls and let them know about the funeral. None of the women had ever met her husband. However, she knew they would want to support her at this time. For the first time, Devin felt that she needed *them* to be there for *her*. All she had was her son, her friends, and her dream.

Devin realized that her decision to work on her dream had come at the right time in her life—just when she would be all alone. Now she had something else to live for.

Jason's funeral was simple. There was only one song: his and Devin's favorite hymn, "Precious Lord." A beautiful poem was read. Then their son, Kevin, did his father's eulogy. The surprising thing was that Devin also spoke about her husband. She spoke of the life they had shared and how much in love they were. The women were all in tears and so sorry they never got the chance to meet Jason. It sounded like he had been a wonderful person, a great husband and father. The ceremony was only about two hours, but it had so much meaning to it.

All of the women were there to support Devin and her son. After the funeral, they all went back to Devin's house and had dinner. There was no sadness, just good friends being together, showing love and support.

Devin felt so blessed to have these women as friends. She loved them all and considered them her family. Her son felt that she had lots of support, and he would not have to worry about her when he went back to New York.

Because of the death of Devin's husband, the women postponed the meeting they had planned to have at Helen's house. Instead, they met on Thursday at the beauty shop. They all felt that this was the place to meet. After all, they were going to be there anyway. Many of their problems, good and bad, had been resolved at Devin's house. The coming together of the boutique had all started at Devin's. So what better place to continue having their meetings?

When all the women arrived at Devin's, she had something she wanted to say to them. "Ladies, I want to thank you for your love and support at this time in my life. If I did not have my son and you guys right now, I don't know what I would do. I loved Jason and I miss him so much. I cannot bear to move his things out of this house, but I know that this is something that I need to do."

Brandi spoke up first. "Devin, you do not have to pack his things by yourself. We will help you or get someone to do it for you. Just let me know."

Devin started crying and hugged Brandi. "That is so thoughtful of you, Brandi. I love you."

Finally they got started with their meeting. The first item on the agenda was a name for the company. Brandi had decided that she wanted to call the company Laurel's House of Design by Brandi. "I wanted to name the shop in honor of Lori, because she has always seen the good in me and knew that I could rise up and be a better person."

That brought tears to all of their eyes. Lori felt honored.

After that, they decided on the officers of their cooperation. Brandi would be the chairman and CEO. Brandi wanted Lori to be president, explaining that she thought Lori was the perfect choice for second in command. All of the women agreed that Lori would be perfect in that position.

Lori said, "We need to talk about this. I will be moving out of state, and that might be a problem."

Brandi said, "Lori, you will be only two hours away by car and twenty minutes by airplane. Therefore, I don't see a problem." Secretly, Brandi was hoping that this would be a reason for Lori to come back. Lori, for her part, was thinking of seeing Laurel's House of Design in one of those swank Atlanta malls.

Yvonne was to be vice president and Christine treasurer. Helen would be in charge of marketing and promotions. They offered Devin a position, but she declined. She told them she was working on a dream of her own, and it was going to be a surprise. However, she was investing $20,000 dollars in Laurel's House of Design, and she handed Brandi the check.

Brandi now had $50,000 dollars for the business, and Christine and Yvonne each invested $25,000 dollars, bringing the total to $100,000 dollars. Lori explained that she and her son were going to invest $50,000 dollars in the business, so now the total was $150,000 dollars. Brandi knew that she would need more, but she had confidence in her plan. She was not worried.

Lori said, "All we need to do is to take our business plan to the bank and secure a line of credit." They decided to talk with Lori's daughter-in-law, a big-shot attorney in Atlanta, and let her advise them on the next move. Their plan had to be solid before they presented it to the bank. All of their figures had to be just right.

Teri, Lori's daughter-in-law, was a smart lawyer who had worked her way up the corporate ladder of a large and very successful company and now was out on her own. She had the high and the low for clients. One of her clients was a former president of the United States—a very popular president at that. Therefore, they knew that they would be safe.

She had put together a top-notch team of lawyers to work with her in her company.

Lori's son was a top businessman who had just sold his company for a very large sum of money. Therefore, they could count on him for good sound advice. He had a Midas touch for smelling out the right moneymaking deals and turning them into fortunes. However, he had given up on business to become a full-time minister. Just as hard as he had worked to be successful in the corporate world, he was now putting all of that energy into building a powerful ministry that was branching out into Africa and other parts of the world. He and Teri were a powerful team. They complemented each other.

Brandi had done a smart thing by surrounding herself with excellent people. This was no accident. She had thought this thing out, and she always knew that these were the people she wanted in her corner. She felt very blessed to have all of these women and their friends and families willing to help her. She would make them proud—and very rich. For the first time in years, she dared to pray and thank God for her blessings.

When the meeting was over, they all proceeded to let Devin make them more beautiful. The mood was lively and festive. Devin could not wait to get back to her writing. Her book was taking shape. Each character was taking on a life of its own. She could hear and feel the characters. If she closed her eyes, she could even see them.

Finally, everyone was gone. It was just Devin, her pad, and her pen. She was now lost in the words forming in her mind. They were taking on a life of their own. She felt exhilarated. *Look out, Oprah, here I come.* She could picture herself on the Oprah show, talking with the great woman herself. Devin could see the whole event taking shape in her mind's eye.

Brandi was so excited about the way things were going. She had a surprise for the women. She had been working on a line of designs for the grand opening of the boutique. She thought it would be great to have a very large charity event to introduce her line of clothing, with part of the proceeds going to a particular charity—and she had one in mind. Brandi had a sister who had AIDS, and she wanted to do an event for AIDS and have AIDS patients wear the clothes in the show. She did not know how this would set with the women, but she was going to tell them and see what they thought.

She knew some beautiful HIV-positive women who did not even look like they were sick. Her sister Charity was doing very well, and if you were not told that she had AIDS, you would never know. Brandi had lost friends to this disease, and she had always wanted to do something to help further education and cure. This could be an opportunity for her to do some good. She took out her pen and pad and started to put her ideas on paper. The more she worked on the idea, the better she liked it.

She could not sleep, so she thought, *I will call Lori and see what she thinks.* When Lori answered, Brandi said, "Lori, I have a great idea, and I could not wait to run it by you. I want to have a charity event to introduce Laurel's House of Design to the city. I want the charity we benefit to be one that help persons with HIV-AIDS." She was so surprised when Lori started to cry. She asked, "Lori, what's wrong?"

Lori said, "I have a daughter who has AIDS also, and I think this is a wonderful idea. My son knows people who can get big names to help."

After Brandi hung up the phone, she got on her knees and prayed. She asked God to forgive her for her past, and she promised God that she would be a better person and asked him to bless all of her friends. She remembered her mother always saying that God was a God of second chances. Brandi knew God had always had a plan for her. She just needed to follow his direction.

Early the next morning, Brandi called the women and asked them to meet with her that afternoon at the Sheraton Hotel in the lobby at six p.m. She had called and reserved a private dining room for them to have a meeting and dinner. She told them to be sure to bring Devin, who was a part of all of this even if she was working on something else.

When they had finished eating, Brandi presented her plan for the fashion show. They all were so surprised and thought it was a great idea.

Helen said, "I know the perfect person to host the show. His name is Rickey Word, the new comedian seen a lot on television. His mother is a member of my church, and I will get her to set up a meeting with him."

The girls all knew about him and were excited at the prospect of getting him to perform. They needed a theme that would encompass the clothing and the whole program. They were all going to think about this and get back together on Friday with their ideas. They really wanted this to be something that would knock the public off their feet and make them open up their pocketbooks for AIDS research.

Lori told them that Teri was coming to town on the weekend to meet with all of them and get them on the right track with setting up their cooperation. Lori had checked into the new mall and had made an appointment to meet with the manager about renting space when she saw a three-story white building in the same area as the mall. She imagined the boutique on the main level with office space on the top level and a beauty shop and spa on the second—all under the name Laurel's House of Design. She took pictures and showed them to the women.

"Our own building. God, this is exciting," said Helen.

Brandi was speechless. Yvonne and Christine were without words for a change. Devin just said, "Wow."

"Do you think we can rent the building?" asked Brandi.

"No," said Lori. "We are going to buy the building. We are going to own that building. There are also rooms we can use to produce your designs. I have contacted the Realtor, and we are going to meet with him tomorrow."

Christine saw this as her chance to help, so she spoke up and said, "I am going to that meeting, and if the price is right, I will back this deal. When the company is a solid company, you can buy the building from me. My late husband left me well-off, and I can afford to purchase the building. So consider it done. My Frank can actually handle the Realtor for us. We are in this together."

Devin spoke up and said, "I am going to invest more than I have, and I will have another check tomorrow."

Brandi had wine served to each woman, and they raised their glasses and gave a toast to Laurel's House of Design by Brandi.

Yvonne went home on cloud nine. She was bubbling over with excitement, and she could not wait to share all of the news with Robert. She open the door calling out his name. He met her in the hallway, and she jumped into his arms. She started telling him all about what she and the girls was planning.

He was so glad to see her all excited about their project. She looked beautiful as she bubbled over with excitement and joy.

She told him, "I have a surprise for you. Get comfortable while I take my bath."

Robert laughed and wondered what she had for him.

Yvonne took her bath in her favorite bath salts. She took her time putting on her makeup and making sure she looked sexy. She took out the red outfit Brandi had given her and put it on. She did not recognize the woman who was looking back at her in the mirror. This woman looked sexy and daring.

She went into the bedroom and dimmed the lights. She put on music and said, "Robert, close your eyes and come into the bedroom." She led him to a chair and told him to sit down. She started the music and said, "Now open your eyes."

He could not believe what he was seeing. She began to make the moves that Brandi had taught her. She could see that he was enjoying every moment of this. She added some moves of her own to the routine, and he grabbed her by the waist and brought her to him. Their eyes locked, and he could see nothing but desire in her eyes. Their lips met, and they melted into one. Robert thought, *I have died and gone to heaven.*

Yvonne thought life could not get any better than this. She whispered, "I love you with all of my heart, Robert, and whatever you need is right here for you."

Robert had never felt so much love for her as he did at that moment. He held her so tight, and they both exploded with ecstasy.

Devin went home and sat for a while, just thinking about all they had discussed. She had finally decided that she could work with the girls now. She would set up the beauty salon and spa. Now they were all involved. However, she would also finish her book—that dream could not die.

She went to her newly purchased computer—a step up from her pad and paper—and started to write. She could feel the words pouring out of her mind onto the screen. The characters had taken on their own personality. She could hear and see them, and she felt their joy as well as their pain.

It was daylight before Devin stopped working on the book. She really felt that life was being good to her and her friends. She missed her husband, and she talked to him all the time, but she was happy in her new life. Working on her book and being involved with the boutique was exciting. She didn't know how she would have been able to handle the loss of her husband if it had not been for her friends and the excitement of her two projects.

She was beginning to think that maybe she should get even more involved in the boutique. The more she thought about that, the more she liked the idea. *Yes*, she thought to herself, *I could get the spa and beauty salon going. A real stylish and elegant spa and salon. I am going to ask the girls if I can have that part of the business to work on.*

Christine was excited about the business, but she had to work on her wedding also. She had two very important things going on at the same time. She wanted everything just right for the wedding. Therefore, she had decided to hire a wedding planner. Frank's daughter had given birth to a beautiful baby girl, and now Frank was ready for them to make plans for the wedding. He was ready to start their life together, and so was she.

The wedding would be in June, which was three months away. The company that Christine had hired assured her that she would have the most beautiful wedding ever—simple but elegant. The wedding reception would be lavish yet very tasteful. Only close family and the girls would be at the wedding ceremony, but everyone was invited to the reception.

Christine had never looked better. She had lost weight, and her hair was simply beautiful. Her eyes glowed and her skin was flawless. She had never been this happy in her entire life.

When Lori and Christine met with the Realtor, they brought along Christine's fiancé, Frank, to help them with the decision. After they had walked every inch of the building, Lori called Brandi and told her to come and see. The Realtor told them that the same person owned the building next door, and they could get that building to use as their warehouse and workshop for machines and workers.

Frank was very proud of the two women; they did not need him here. They handled the whole deal themselves, and the Realtor realized that he was dealing with business-savvy women. They had done their homework and knew what they were doing.

Brandi drove up to the front of the building and just sat in her car staring at the building. In her mind's eye, she could see the fitting rooms and the beautiful decorated interior. This place was perfect, and as she sat there, tears began to stream down her face. In that moment, she knew that her dreams were coming to life.

Helen, Devin, and Yvonne drove up behind her, and they watched her with a smile on their faces. They all got out of their cars and went inside the building. Each saw the potential in the property, and they all agreed on the purchase of both properties.

Laurel's House of Design was on its way.

As with many deals, however, there was a hitch. The women had the money and the credit, but there was something about them that did not sit well with some of the locals: they were six black women wanting to get prime real estate in an area where there were no black businesses. The other retailers in the area were worried that they would not come up to neighborhood standards. They had heard that one of the women was a stripper. So they joined together to block the sale of the building.

Brandi became very angry about this discrimination. She called a meeting with the ladies to discuss the situation. "I am not going to allow these people's prejudice to stop my plans," said Brandi. "I was a stripper, not anymore. We all have been something in our past lives. I will not let this stop me."

"I agree," said Lori.

"What shall we do?" asked Helen.

"I know what we'll do," said Lori. "We will set up a meeting with the locals and the mayor; if necessary, we will go to the city council. We will tell them our goals for the business, and we will proceed with our plans whether they like it or not."

"I agree," said Helen. "We all agree. We will fight for this dream."

The women could not get a private meeting, so they decided to go before the city council and bring their case out in the open. Lori became their spokesperson.

"I am here to tell you that Laurel's House of Design will be the most exclusive boutique that this town has ever seen. Designs by Brandi will make our place unique. I have brought a few items to show you. We will add to the prestige of the area, and we are catering to everyone. We have the financing and the desire and ambition to make Laurel's a very unique addition to the area. We have big plans, and we will succeed.

"We do not have the time to waste fighting to buy the property," she continued. "We need to get started, and we want your blessing on the sale of the building to us. Otherwise, we will take our plan to Atlanta, and Birmingham will be left out again. I thank you for your time, and I hope we can begin in an atmosphere of cooperation." She did not bring up the stripper gossip, and they did not asked her about it.

The council voted to allow the group to purchase the property and was excited about the venture.

"Lori, you are awesome," said Brandi.

"We all toast you," said Devin.

They thanked God that they had overcome this hurdle. They said a prayer of thanks. They knew He was opening doors for them, and they were following His lead.

Before the month was over, they had completed the deal for the purchase of the buildings and had all of their legal work for their corporation completed. Things were beginning to move quite fast.

Brandi was busy working on her designs. The women had decided that the theme of the fashion show would be the beauty of life. Everything would celebrate life. Since AIDS knew no gender, race, or age, Brandi was designing outfits from sportswear to evening wear. The next step was to get models for the show. They had decided to have the gala at the town's civic center.

Lori knew a member of the board for the civic center, and when she told him about the show, he got the center to donate the building for that night for the sum of one dollar. Brandi could not believe the things these women could accomplish.

Helen was working on getting their building ready to use. She was totally in charge of the decorating. Brandi had only two requests: double mahogany doors and a beautifully decorated front window—just like she had seen it in her dreams.

Brandi had final say on all decorations for the boutique. They all wanted it to be just as Brandi had dreamed it could be. After all, this was her dream, and they were just along for the ride. All of the women had started out thinking they were helping Brandi. But they had started to wonder just who was helping whom.

It had been a very hectic week, and all of the women were ready to relax at Devin's. One by one, they entered the shop. They just wanted to relax and get some pampering done.

Brandi and Lori were working on a surprise for Christine for the wedding. Lori had purchased the material, and Brandi had designed Christine's wedding attire.

"I am having the hardest time finding what I want in a wedding dress, and I do not have much time," said Christine. "I don't know what I'm going to do."

Brandi eased out of the room, went to her car, and brought in her sketchpad. "Christine, I have something I want you to see," said Brandi.

When Christine saw the drawing of the dress, she could not believe her eyes. It was stunning—a beautiful jacket with a long skirt. The lines of the outfit were just right. Brandi explained the details of the suit and the warm creamy color. Then she showed the headpiece. Christine was so excited.

Christine knew this was the only outfit she would want to wear on her special day. Brandi assured her that it would be ready in plenty of time for the wedding. She would need some fittings, but there would be no problems.

"I have picked the jewelry," said Helen, and she got it out for Christine to see. The jewelry was beautiful, and again the tears started flowing from each of them. Devin would do Christine's hair for the big day, and Yvonne had something old for her. They told her not to worry about the wedding—it was going to be beautiful.

The wedding now taken care of, the women went on to the next thing, which was what they were going to wear to the wedding and where the honeymoon was going to be. Christine said that she and Frank had decided to only go off for the weekend and take a long trip after they had opened the boutique and had the fashion show.

Brandi could not believe that Christine would put her honeymoon off for this. She jumped up, hugging and thanking Christine for all she was doing.

Yvonne said, "Enough of this crying, let's talk about Lori. Are you still going to move to Atlanta?"

Lori smiled and said, "That's a done deal. I am moving, but I am not ready to go until after we get this project up and running. I am committed to all of you and our boutique, spa, and salon."

Devin finally spoke up and said, "What do you ladies think about my working on the spa and salon for the boutique?" They all said it is about time she stepped forward. Devin started laughing, for she realized that they had been hoping she would want to do just that.

Finally, every member had her role to play in the project. Devin would start researching the different spas and salons all over and see what would fit into their style. They knew that they wanted everything to be top-of-the-line and elegant.

The women were at Devin's until after midnight, but as usual, it had been a very good evening. They had made Christine happy and had gotten a definite commitment out of Devin, and it was what they had all wanted. Lord, what that woman could do with a curling iron was special. They knew she would have the finest salon and spa in the state or the country.

Their goal was to eventually spread out to Atlanta and even further. *If you are going to dream, then dream big* was their motto. They were not afraid of stepping out to win.

CHAPTER 7

The renovation of the building was almost complete. Helen had put all of her time and energy into working with the design team she had hired. One smart thing she had done was to go to the head of the architectural and design school at the university and make a deal with the head of the department to use the building as a project for the brightest and smartest students to work on. The students toured the building and talked with the women, and then they went back to their drawing boards and each designed the building as they thought it should be. All of the designs would then be presented to the women to choose the best design for the boutique.

In a month, all of the students presented their designs based on the women's dreams for the building. One of the students' designs really grabbed their hearts and souls, capturing the very essence of the dream. The student's name was Sarah Brown. She was from Georgia, going to school in Alabama.

Now, after all the designing and work, the interior was really something to see. It looked like a Paris boutique, with gilded chairs and settees, chandeliers hanging from the ceilings, and carpets so plush it felt as if you were walking on air. Beautiful art hung on the walls. There was a runway where a customer could have outfits modeled for her so she could decide which one she wanted. The dressing rooms were spacious and comfortable, each with its own settees. The clients—those special customers who could afford the very best—would be served wine and cheese as they had a private showing.

Then there was the rack floor where the clothes were made and designed in good taste for women on a budget. The colors of the walls were warm and cozy. Music would flow throughout.

The salon area was beautiful. No woman would ever be seen getting her hair shampooed, colored, and relaxed. All of the prep was behind closed doors. No bowls or dryers were in the front of the salon. The waiting area was very chic, with comfortable chairs, televisions, a juice bar, wine, and cheese. Devin decided to add a nursery for women who had to bring their children along. This area was nice and colorful, with all the items needed to keep children busy. She hired a very good person to watch them.

As you entered the spa area, you could hear running water from all of the fountains and soft, very relaxing music. The area was geared toward relaxation. The colors were warm and soothing. Soft plush towels and bathrobes awaited the clients. The women went all out but not overboard on the spending. Many beautiful things, like the artwork on the walls, were on loan to them from a friend who had his own art studio. They called on favors from friends and associates who they had helped in the past.

The boutique was located in a very upscale community. Potential clients were mostly young and married to rich or well-off husbands. Those husbands were corporate types, and money and prestige were uppermost in their minds. Everyone kept an eye on the shop, and there was much speculation about what kind of place it would be.

There was a rumor that a very famous person owned the shop and that it was going to be the fanciest place in town. The women loved all the rumors and excitement that the shop was generating. They knew that rumors and curiosity would bring in the crowds and that they would have to live up to the hype to keep those customers. They left nothing to chance. Beautiful engraved invitations for the fashion show went out to all of the town's elite, as well as to different organizations. They had a plan, and they had no doubt that it would work.

There was going to be quite a lot of press, because Helen had promised her friend at the paper an exclusive story about the women, and Brandi in particular. Brandi was fine with this—she figured that a little notoriety would help. She knew that the fashion show was the key to the boutique's grand opening.

After months of hard work, the time for the fashion show was fast approaching. The women had asked Beverly Stokes, the owner of a modeling school in the city, to work with the models. Brandi had handpicked all of the models herself. They were all very pretty, and they had one thing in common: they were all HIV-positive. Lori's daughter was one of the models, and she was so excited about all of the attention she was getting. They had chosen handsome young men to escort the women to the runway.

On the night of the show, one of the hottest new comedians in the country would be performing, as well as a full orchestra thanks to the citywide concert orchestra. Brandi had designed all of the outfits, and she had gotten more than enough help with the making of each one. Many of the fabrics had been donated by various companies and stores that knew what a good cause this was. AIDS had affected many families, and they were eager to help make this a success. Brandi had never worked so hard in her life, but she knew that it was going to be worth it.

The decorations were being handled by the best party decorator in the city, and he had donated his time and the decorations, as he had lost many friends to the AIDS virus. Many people volunteered their services when they were approached to help because they wanted to help HIV-AIDS patients in any way and contribute to AIDS research.

The big night had finally arrived. Brandi knew that the success or failure of this event would determine the outcome of the rest of her plans. Everyone had been working nonstop to get to this moment. There was so much excitement backstage. Devin had all of the models in a room with her, and of course she had plenty of help. Several stylists had donated their time. A makeup artist for a very popular cosmetics line and his team were doing makeup. Then the ladies were sent to the dressing room where they would put on Brandi's beautiful creations.

Lori and Helen were everywhere, giving orders and talking constantly. Christine pulled all of the women into a room and said a prayer for the success of the show. Again, she had surprised the women with her actions.

Brandi went into the main room and could not believe how beautiful all the decorations were. She walked the runway and allowed herself to visualize the night and how it would turn out. She felt good vibes, and her inner spirit let her know that everything was going to be wonderful. She silently said a prayer of thanks to God for allowing her to be blessed with such wonderful friends.

They only made one change in the program. They all decided that Lori was going to be host and emcee for the evening. Lori hesitated at first, but they convinced her that she was the perfect person for the job. Therefore, Brandi had also designed different outfits for Lori to wear all throughout the show. She would be changing outfits several times. Brandi had created dresses for each of the women to wear, as well as one for herself. Devin did all of their hair. Everything had been done that needed to be done. It was just a matter now of carrying out the plan.

By seven p.m., the guests were all in their seats, and the house was packed as the lights came on, the curtain to the stage opened, and Lori walked out to the mike. The applause was loud and long. Lori looked beautiful. Her gray hair was perfect—not a strand out of place. Her makeup was flawless.

However, the showstopper was the gown she was wearing. It was gray in color, a light cool shade. Lori's hair and the dress were the same color. The dress seemed molded to her body and then began to flare out at the bottom with a train following behind her. There was a split in the front of the dress that was not too revealing but showed that she had a good pair of legs. There were diamonds glittering all over the dress, and the lights caused then to sparkle and shimmer. She had on matching gloves and shoes. The way the light shined on Lori enhanced her good looks and made her more glamorous

Lori was in her element. She welcomed everyone to the show and told them the idea behind it, which was to raise awareness and money for AIDS research and education. Then the show began. Each outfit and each model was more beautiful than the one before.

Once the show was over, the bidding for the outfits began. The women were in shock at how quickly and for how much the beautiful outfits were going. This was more than they had hoped for. After all, Brandi was an unknown designer with no formal training or big name backing her.

At the end of the evening, Lori introduced Brandi to the audience, and the house went wild. Brandi had designed her own beautiful outfit, including a long coat with a hood. As Lori began telling the story of Brandi and her dream, Brandi walked further out onto the stage in this beautiful gold lamé gown and coat. Her hair had gold highlights in it. Her tawny complexion was made up to look as if she had on no makeup. She was stunning. The dress she was wearing complimented her to perfection.

Lori had decided to talk about Brandi's background. A friend in the media told her it was best to have all the little secrets out in the open, so nothing could come back to harm them later. It only made Brandi that much more mysterious and glamorous in the eyes of the public. Lori told the audience of Brandi's desire to help in the fight against AIDS by using her God-given talent for this benefit and to show the world what she was capable of doing.

Lori was sure that nothing from Brandi's past would matter now. Therefore, she told the story in her own way, and when Brandi walked to the mike, the crowd gave her a standing ovation. The night was Brandi's, and Lori faded into the background. Lori and the women were so proud of Brandi and her accomplishments.

Brandi introduced all of the models and spoke to the crowd with compassion in her voice as she explained that all of the beautiful models were dealing with HIV. "However, the disease has not stopped them from living the good life that they wanted, because they are all fighters. I understand their plight, because I am a fighter also. Dreams do come true, and tonight is just the beginning of my dreams coming true.

"I want to introduce all of the people who helped Laurel's House of Design put on this show, and I thank all of the people who have given more than just their money but their time and love as well. Now I want the rest of my partners to come to the stage. Helen, Devin, Yvonne, Christine, and Lori." She told the crowd how they had believed in her and made everything happen for her.

The show was a huge success. Lori announced the grand opening of the boutique. They all knew it would be a success too.

There was a cocktail party after the show in the private club of the civic center. All of the town's elite came. They began asking for appointments to be seen by Brandi at the boutique. Many of the women wanted originals that no one else would be wearing. All of the gowns in the show had been sold. Buyers were seeking to purchase Lori's and Brandi's outfits off their backs. Brandi decided there would never be more than two of any dress on a rack, and special designs for certain clients would be a part of the beauty of the boutique.

Finally, the night was over, and the women all gathered at Devin's. They could not go home without getting together alone and just quietly taking in all the happenings of the night. They had raised over $250,000 dollars for AIDS, and all of the money was going to the charity.

Devin finally said, "Ladies, this has been the best night ever probably for any of us. Now we can get the boutique open and get Christine married off before that man changes his mind. So ladies, let us drink to success."

Then each woman went to her own home to dream the rest of the night away.

Two months after the fashion show came the grand opening of the boutique. The success of the fashion show was still being talked about. People were calling from the entertainment community wanting to meet Brandi and see her designs. The designs had been a huge success, and the opening was going to be another mind-blowing event. It had taken a year of hard work and planning, but it was worth the time and effort to accomplish what they wanted.

The night before the opening of the boutique, all of the women walked every inch of the building. They wanted to make sure that everything was in place. It looked like a French store. There were no racks in the VIP area. Those persons would have their clothes modeled for them, and the designs would be brought out for their approval even before the clothes were put on a model.

The rack area for the less-expensive items was handled with great care to maintain that elegant feeling. There were only four racks, and the walls had shelves of beautiful sweaters and blouses in all colors. There was a foundation area as well. Everything was done in excellent taste. This area had a juice bar and beautiful dressing rooms that were spacious and comfortable, so persons in that area felt like VIPs also.

The spa was done in a Roman style. There was a large pool with columns and private rooms for massages. There was marble everywhere, along with large candleholders and gilded-style stools and chairs. Devin had outdone herself on the spa.

The beauty salon was done in stainless steel and black. It had a futuristic look about it. Everything was shiny and elegant-looking. The salon and spa had juice bars and fruit. After the women had walked the salon several times and made a few changes, the place was ready for the public. They felt very proud of their accomplishments, and they gave Helen all the credit for the look of the place. She had paid attention to even the smallest of details.

The office area was tastefully decorated, and the conference room was already hosting its first big meeting. The women were all seated around the table, and they vowed to have a charity fashion show each year to introduce Brandi's new designs. They also decided that they were going to look for the most talented young people in the field of design and business to work with them. Brandi would look for new designers in the different schools who had the talent to carry themselves to the top of the design world and stay there.

For now, however, the friends just wanted to relax for a moment and have an attitude of gratefulness. They thanked each other for what each brought to the team. They stood in a circle and gave thanks to God for what He was doing in their lives. They knew that none of this had just happened. It had been divine intervention. They gave thanks to God for giving them favor. They hugged each other and called it a night, for they knew they had a big day tomorrow.

At eleven a.m., the opening ceremony for Laurel's House of Design by Brandi began. The mayor's wife, Gladys Barton, performed the ribbon-cutting. She was a socialite who had been brought up in the tightknit society of the city. Her father and his father had been mayors and governors of the city and state. If she approved of something, then all the bluebirds wanted in, and she loved the outfits that Brandi had designed especially for her. So all the women with money came calling.

As the first customers entered the boutique, they could not believe how elegant it was. They toured the entire building. There were tuxedo-dressed well-built young men passing out champagne. There were men and women in togas taking appointments for the spa. There were receptionists taking appointments for the salon.

In the VIP area, there was a private showing of new designs that would be one-of-a-kind. Others checked out the area for women who did not have a lot of money to throw around but wanted to look elegant also. They were shown the different styles and told that they would never see more than two of any one style on the rack. They would not have to worry about seeing themselves all over town. In this way, the boutique captured the hearts of the rich and working women as well as the stay-at-home moms, who particularly appreciated the nursery.

The grand opening was a success. Each area of the business had many appointments, and the rack area was going to be busy also. After the shop had closed for the day, the women went back to Devin's to laugh and talk about the event. They always ended up in Devin's basement. They had decided that this would be their base, and no one would be able to interfere with their time at Devin's. Thursday was still on for them.

CHAPTER 8

The opening had been a huge success like the fashion show before it, and the boutique was up and running. Before anything else could be accomplished, Christine had to have her wedding. She had put Frank on hold long enough, and she did not want to lose this man. Therefore, the time had come for the ceremony to take place.

Two weeks before the big day, Christine's dress was ready, and all the arrangements had been taken care of. A week later, Frank's daughter and her family arrived, and they were staying at Frank's house. Christine and Frank had not told anyone that they had decided to sell both houses and buy one that was their very own. They had found the perfect place on the lake. The house was beautiful, and they had both fallen in love with it.

The lake was private and filled with swans. The grounds of the house were manicured to perfection. There was a pool and a guesthouse on the property and a studio. To show the house off, they had moved the reception to the house. Everyone's invitation to the reception had an address, but no one knew that the place was the couple's new home. Not even the gang knew. How surprised they would be!

The wedding of Christine and Frank took place on a beautiful Saturday. The bride was lovely in her wedding ensemble designed by Brandi of Laurel's House of Design. The bride had one matron of honor, who was the groom's daughter; the groom's son-in- law was his best man.

Christine looked into Frank's eyes as she spoke her vows. "Frank, since I met you, my whole world has changed. I feel so much love for you, and I want to spend the rest of my life loving you and making you happy."

Frank said, "I love you more than life itself. I pledge to make you happy and to love you forever. I am so proud that you will be my wife."

The minister said, "I now pronounce you husband and wife. You may kiss your wife." All the women were in tears and so happy for their friend.

The reception followed the wedding at an elegant home on a private lake filled with swans. There were tents all over the grounds, decorated in beautiful colors, with food and music. Champagne fountains and handsome waiters and servers catered to the guests' every need.

It was beautiful as night began to fall and the moon shimmered on the lake. The bride and groom went out, got into a boat, and rowed around the lake as their favorite singer serenaded them. Then a limo pulled onto the grounds to carry the happy couple to the airport for their trip. Before they got into the limo, they thanked everyone for being there, and then they announced that they had bought the property and that all of them had been their first houseguests. Off they went for their private time together.

After Christine and Frank left the reception, Lori, Helen, Devin, Brandi, and Yvonne found a quiet place to sit and rest a while. They were all so happy for Christine and Frank, for their marriage and their beautiful new home. The six friends had accomplished so many things during the past year, and they had other plans on the drawing board.

Lori had put off her move, and now she felt it was time for her to relocate to Atlanta. They had all thought that Lori was going to forget about the move now that they had so much going on. However, it was still in the back of her head to go to Atlanta. She had decided that she was going to keep a place in Birmingham so that when she came to town, she would have her own private place to live.

She was going to keep on working with the girls, but she had to do this, make this move. She had to know whether she could live there. It had been her dream for so long. There was so much more to her dream that she had not confided to anyone.

CHAPTER 9

Six months had passed, and the boutique was really doing well. Christine had settled into her new home and was working overtime decorating it. Yvonne and Robert were spending a lot of time on their marriage and business interests. Helen had settled into her job with Brandi and was now very happy with her life and the way things were working out. Devin had the spa and salon going full speed. Both stayed booked, with clients on the waiting list to get in.

Devin had not abandoned her other dream of writing a book. Every moment she could spare, she worked on the book. She even worked on it on her computer in her office at the boutique. It was finally finished, and she was about to send it to a publisher to find out just how good it was. She had no doubt in her mind that the book would be a hit. It would not be long now before Ms. Oprah herself would be calling her to be on the Oprah show.

However, tonight they all had another appointment that was sad for them. Lori was having her going-away party. It was a very private affair, just Lori's family and a few special friends getting together. They all hated to see her move to Atlanta.

To everyone's surprise, Brandi was taking it the hardest. Lori was so proud of all that Brandi had accomplished. She was being written up in all the fashion magazines, and some of the most famous people around were now wearing her clothes. Last month, Brandi was in Paris buying fabric and meeting some of the world's greatest designers. She visited all of the famous design houses and came home excited, already working on her next line.

A second boutique had opened, and it was doing extremely well. It was located in Buckhead in Atlanta, and Lori would be in and out making sure it stayed on track. Still, Brandi did not want to see Lori leave. The evening was festive, but the women's hearts were not in it.

After dinner, Lori stood and said, "I want to thank all of you for your love and friendship. I will only be two hours and a phone call away. One Thursday out of each month, I will meet at Devin's for our evening of beauty treatments and fun." They would not give up their Thursdays, no matter how famous or rich they became.

They kept the last Thursday of the month as their time to go back to where it had all started—Devin's basement. That kept them grounded, and they would evaluate the month and discuss everything as they had always done.

Lori said, "All of you are so important to me, and you all will always be a part of my life." Lori raised her glass to them and made a toast, saying, "You ladies are my soul sisters—meaning, we are glued together for life."

Brandi started crying. "Oh, Lori, you are more than a friend to me." Lori had become her mentor and mother figure. Brandi did not ever want to lose her friend. She felt that Lori was the glue that was helping to hold her together. They hugged and shed tears and enjoyed this last evening together. Lori was all packed and was leaving the next day. She would be back in a month. Finally, the party was over and each woman gave Lori her final good-bye.

Lori's move to Atlanta had been smooth. Lori thanked God for all of the things that had happened in her life over the past few months, and all the time since she had separated from her husband. Sometimes she felt that all of this was too good to be true.

She had moved into a townhouse with her sister. It was the first time she had ever lived outside of her hometown. It was a bit intimidating to her. Atlanta was so much faster than Birmingham. Traffic was frightening. She saw that she had many adjustments to make. However, being that this was the world she wanted to fit into, she was willing to make any necessary adjustments.

Atlanta reminded her of New York City. She was so impressed with New York. Everything was so large and moving so fast. That's the way Atlanta felt to her. The first thing she had to conquer was her fear of traffic as she learned her way around the city.

Well, the only way to handle fear is to meet it head-on, Lori said to herself. *Traffic, here I come.* She headed out the door to her car, smiling happily.

Lori had decided that the best way to learn her way around was to hit the streets and drive. That was what she was going to do on this day. She started out on her journey, and the first thing she wanted to do was find the boutique on Buckhead. It took her three hours to get there, but finally she drove up to the boutique. In trying to find it, she found many other places she would need to go in the future. The traffic was not that frightening after she started driving in it. She also realized that as soon as she learned her way around, driving in the traffic would not be that scary to her.

She parked her car and went into the boutique. An attractive young woman greeted her as soon as she entered the shop. "Good evening, my name is Angela. Welcome to Laurel's. May I help you today?"

Lori decided to act as if she was a customer. "Yes, young lady, you may." She wanted to go though the experience that the customers would have. Therefore, she did not tell the woman that she was one of the owners.

"I am most happy to help you. What is your name, please?"

"My name is Mrs. Farrell," Lori said.

"Mrs. Farrell, let me take you to the showroom," said Angela.

Lori told her that she was interested in seeing the latest and best that Laurel's had to offer. The young woman seated her in a private room and introduced her to a young woman named Stacey. "Mrs. Farrell, this is Stacey, and she will help you with your selections." They offered her wine and cheese. Lori declined, and they immediately went to the juice bar and asked her what would she like.

Lori was impressed. "Do you have seltzer water?"

"Yes, we have that."

"Then I will have seltzer water."

After serving Lori her beverage, Stacey asked, "Mrs. Farrell, are you interested in seeing casual, business, dressy, or formal wear?"

Lori explained to Stacey that she wanted to see all of the lines. "I am interested in changing my look, and I want some clothes that will reflect that change." She saw that Stacey was looking at her closely; she was dressed in a very smart suit by Chanel. Her hair did not have a strand out of place.

After carefully looking Lori over, Stacey began to ask some questions. "May I ask, what are your favorite colors? What type of business are you in? Do you travel and entertain a lot, Mrs. Farrell?"

Lori answered as honestly as she could without giving away her identity. Stacey then asked Lori to excuse her while she went and picked out some selections.

Lori was very impressed with Stacey and could not wait to see what she would bring out. While Lori waited, she took out her planner and began to make notes of the things and places that she wanted to go and do. She intended to check out all of the best stores and boutiques that the city had to offer. She wanted to make sure that none of them was topping Laurel's. The boutique must stay in a class by itself. She liked the atmosphere of the shop, and it was decorated in elegant taste— thanks to the standards that Helen had set for the boutiques.

Within a short time, Stacey returned and began having models come out wearing one fabulous outfit after another. Lori was so surprised that Stacey had picked clothing that was meant for her. The colors were perfect for her, and she had Lori's taste down pat. Before Lori knew it, she had picked several outfits to purchase.

She could see that Stacey was very pleased and proud of herself. She could also see that the young woman enjoyed what she was doing. Lori had nothing but praise for her. Finally, she told Stacey who she was and that the outfits she had picked were going home with her.

Stacey liked Lori and was not at all upset that she had allowed them to think that she was just another client. She showed Lori around the boutique and introduced her to all the employees. Stacey told Lori she was in school for design and her goal was to become a fashion designer in the future. Lori promised to introduce her to Brandi. Then she left the shop, as Stacey was having her clothes sent to her home. Lori could not wait to report to the girls that the Atlanta shop was safe and that she would be there a lot.

Lori's next stop was going to be her daughter-in-law's firm. She knew that it was downtown, and Stacey had given her good directions to the Peachtree Plaza office complex. She finally saw the building. She was about to turn into the parking deck when she saw that the building had valet parking. Therefore, she drove to the front of the building and gave her keys to the attendant. He informed her that the office she was looking for was on the fourteenth floor. She got on the elevator, and it was like being in a jet. It whisked her to the fourteenth floor so fast that her head was spinning.

The doors of the elevator opened, and she stepped out into the foyer of the law offices. The entire fourteenth floor belonged to the law firm of Watts and Morgan. The young woman at the desk asked her who she wanted to see, and when she realized that this was Teri Watts's mother-in-law, Lori was escorted to a beautifully decorated room and told to have a seat. Coffee, tea, and other refreshments were made available. After twenty minutes, a young man came and escorted her to Teri's office. It was very spacious and tastefully decorated.

Teri got up from behind her desk and greeted Lori. "How are you enjoying Atlanta?"

"Great. However, this traffic takes some getting used to," Lori told her.

Teri laughed. "You will get used to it."

"I hope so," Lori replied. "I have had a very good day, Teri. I am so happy with the people who are running the shop downtown. I love the atmosphere. You know what? I want to have a charity event here in Atlanta that will benefit AIDS research. I want to have a party and invite Atlanta's elite."

She knew that her son and daughter-in-law were entrenched in the elite circle of the city. Lori wanted to meet these people and cultivate friendships. She wanted them to buy clothes from Laurel's and have Brandi design just for them. Teri thought it was a good idea. As they talked about it, ideas began to flow.

The party became a charity event with a fashion show put on by Laurel's, sponsored by the Watts and Morgan law firm, with designs by Brandi. This event would also benefit the AIDS foundation in Atlanta. Only this time, they were going to use professional models and entertainers. Teri gave Lori the names of the top professionals in Atlanta to help put this affair over, and she told Lori to throw her name around for any favors needed. Teri also gave Lori office space and a secretary to work with her.

Lori hurried home to call the ladies and tell them of her plans. They had a conference call, and Lori told them what she was planning and how it all came about. They were all very impressed and excited. It meant they would all be visiting Atlanta.

Brandi told Lori that she was working on new designs that could be unveiled at the fashion show. Lori told Brandi about Stacey and that the young woman wanted to meet her and show her some designs. Brandi told Lori that she had arranged to spend time studying with a very famous designer to improve her craft. She didn't want to be just good—Brandi wanted to be the very best. Lori was happy to hear about Brandi's plan and told her that it was a wise decision.

They talked over a few more business details, and then Devin told them that she would have a surprise for them when they met on the last Thursday of the month. They tried to get it out of her, but she would not say another word. They finally hung up with a final "See you on Thursday at Devin's."

Lori was settling in and beginning to feel at home in Atlanta. She got up every morning and went into the office that Teri was allowing her to use. Not only was she working on the charity event, she was starting a foundation for teenagers with HIV. Then she decided to include all age groups of women of color with HIV. She had long thought that there was a need for more education in the black community on HIV among women of color. She knew that the number of black women with the disease was increasing.

Lori decided that this was one of her missions in life—to help as many women as she possibly could remain free of AIDS. She was talking to doctors and others, asking them to show her what her foundation could do to help. She was surprised at how receptive people in the medical profession were to her and her cause. Lori knew firsthand how AIDS not only affected patients but also their loved ones. She knew that the patients had to be treated with meds and the family would need some kind of therapy and counseling to help them cope with the disease and what it could do. Lori knew this because she was a mother with concern for her own child with AIDS.

Lori was working with women of color because she felt they were the ones who were being forgotten and suffering the most. She was getting pamphlets and speakers to go into the schools and churches to talk to young women. She also had an idea for a women's conference on AIDS for teenagers, young adults, and adult women, bringing in medical professionals and entertainers to speak with them. She would also get AIDS patients themselves to tell their stories.

So Lori was really busy, and she was trying to stay busy so she could not and would not have to think about how lonely she was for companionship and how much she wished that the man she loved would love her enough to change his life and live the rest of his years with her. She did not believe that it would happen, so she stayed busy so she would not feel the pain and the hurt.

Finally it was the last Thursday of the month, and they were all meeting at Devin's. It was no longer easy for them to get together like this. They were all so busy now with the business and their private lives. All day long, Devin had been anticipating this time. She hoped that Lori would make it in. She had so much to tell the girls, and she needed to do it before they read or heard about it in the press or on some television show.

They had planned to be at Devin's at three p.m. It was only one p.m. when Devin heard the doorbell. When she opened the door, there stood Lori. They were so glad to see each other. After they had exchange pleasantries, Lori told Devin that she had come early so they could talk for a while before the others got there. Devin saw the sadness in Lori's eyes for just a moment, and then it went away. Devin decided to throw caution to the wind and asked Lori why she seemed so sad at times.

The question caught Lori off guard, and the tears began to roll down her face. "I wish more than anything in the world that I could spend the rest of my life with my husband and be happy. However, I know that I cannot do that, because he will never change his ways. I am lonely for companionship, and I will never get a divorce because I cannot bring myself to finalize the end of the marriage. It would be like saying that I had wasted forty years of my life with this man. I cannot bring myself to do that." Just as quickly as the tears had come, she dried them up and told Devin that she was okay with her life and was going to make the rest of it mean something. She had six wonderful children, so the first half of her life had not been in vain.

Finally, one by one, the other women arrived. Christine came through the door glowing with happiness. She looked so good—just radiant. Yvonne was the surprise: she had cut her hair and was dressed very smart and fashionable. You could tell she was very happy with her life. Helen was bubbling over with enthusiasm and looking very good herself. Brandi was the picture of sophistication and elegance. She did not favor the young stripper who had come on Thursdays and had that *I do not give a damn* attitude. That Brandi was gone. Lori was so happy to see them all, and they were happy to see her.

Lori took a hard look at Devin as she was serving them refreshments. There was something different about her. Devin was a very good-looking woman, but there was something else. Lori could not put her finger on it. They were all laughing and talking at the same time, just like a bunch of teenage girls.

Devin finally said, "Okay, ladies, let's take care of any business we need to take care of, and then we will have some fun." They all agreed to that.

Brandi started the meeting by telling the women about where she saw the company going. She and Helen had reports to present on the financial picture of the business, which was very good. They were now in a position to purchase the buildings from Christine.

Brandi had identified Miami, New York, and California as the next areas for Laurel's to expand into. She felt the boutique in California would have to be on Rodeo Drive in Beverly Hills. She also wanted to make the boutiques even more upscale, and the women all agreed they would need the very best to work on the new shops.

They decided that California would be the area to open in next. Christine and Helen would go out there and see what was available. They would contact a Realtor in Beverly Hills to help with the location.

Devin followed with a report on the spa and salon. Both were doing great and grossing excellent revenue. She also had great ideas for improvement. Everyone was happy about how well things were going.

Next, Lori gave them a report on how the charity ball and fashion show was coming along. This time they were allowing an event planner to do the work. They were less personally involved in this affair than they had been on the first one. Other people were asking to have a hand this time around.

When Lori told them about the foundation, they all volunteered to help in any way they could. Christine reported that she was looking at property for the company to buy. She explained that she wanted them to do some things in the inner-city neighborhoods that would provide jobs as well as affordable items to buy. They all thought that was a wonderful idea. They had long known that they wanted to introduce inner-city girls to the world of fashion design. They were going to give back as much as they could in time and money. Each woman wrote Lori a nice check for the foundation, as Lori had used her own money to start it.

Finally, all of the business was over, and Brandi asked Devin about her surprise Devin got up and went into another room. When she came back, she had her hands behind her back. Slowly she brought her hands out into the open, and she was holding a book. She held it up so they could see the cover. There was a drawing of six women along with the words "*Sisters Who Are Sisters Born of the Soul* by Devin Hampton."

She passed the book around, and each woman read the dedication. The book was dedicated to all of them and the love they had for each other. She gave each woman a signed copy to read before it hit the stores. She had decided to give half the proceeds to Lori's foundation. She told them that she had no doubt the book would be a best seller, and her publishers agreed. They were going to put a lot of promotion behind the book, and one day she was going to be on the Oprah show. They were all in the book under different names.

Brandi said, "If you wrote about us and all that has gone on with us, the book will sell millions. My part will sell a million by itself!"

Christine said, "No, Brandi, my part can sell two million!" They all laughed.

The women raised their glasses and gave a toast to Devin and the success of her book.

Yvonne said, "I hope you all will remember that I contributed to the book."

Helen said, "Well, ladies, I know that I am sensational in the book."

They were laughing so hard they didn't notice that Lori wasn't joining in. Finally she said, "I am so boring that I could not possibly be in the book."

Brandi almost choked on her drink. "Lori, you must be kidding! You know you are in the book, and it is not boring."

"Here, here!" they all said as they finished their drinks.

They decided to order in dinner so they could continue to let their hair down and enjoy themselves without the scrutiny of the public. Christine called Frank and told him she would be late, and Yvonne called Robert and told him she was with the women and that it might be a long night. Helen and Brandi did not have to call anyone. They dated, but they were not getting serious about anyone anytime soon.

The women talked and made plans late into the night. About two in the morning, they finally said good night and parted for their homes. Lori had kept a small place to live in when she came to town, but Brandi invited Lori to stay at her place and Lori agreed. Helen went home and fell into her bed, dreaming of bigger things to come. Yvonne could not wait to get home so she could keep Robert up the rest of the night, and that is exactly what she did.

When Christine got home, she found that Frank had been reading in bed, gotten sleepy, and fallen asleep. She tip-toed over to the bed and kissed him on the cheek. He turned over, opened his eyes, and said, "You get more beautiful every day."

She smiled and said, "This is the reason I keep you here, just so you can build my ego up."

They both laughed and he told her to hurry and get in bed.

"Yes sir," she said and dived into bed.

Lori and Brandi arrived at Brandi's new home and checked on her son and the housekeeper. Then they sat in the den discussing the charity event in Atlanta and the new stores they were getting ready to open, as well as the foundation. They had so much going on.

Lori asked Brandi if she was happy. Brandi told her she had never been this happy in her life. She had known that she would one day make a turnaround in her life and that it would be big. She had never lost her dream to own her own business. Now, her life was beginning to exceed even her wildest dreams. She told Lori that there were others out there dreaming just as she had done, and she wanted to give back by helping others make their dreams come true.

Lori was so proud of Brandi. Her eyes were glowing, and you could feel the peace and contentment in her life. "What about a man?" Lori asked. "Do you have any desire to build a relationship with someone?"

"Believe it or not," Brandi told Lori, "I do feel that in the future I am going to want someone in my life who will love my son and me. I am not in a hurry, and when I meet that person, I will know it and I will give in to it."

"You have come a long way, and I am so proud of you," Lori said. "But now I am going to go to bed and rest some."

"Wait a minute," said Brandi. "You are not going to get away without answering some of *my* questions. What about you, Lori, are you happy? Is working enough for you? Do you not want a man in your life?"

Lori became very quiet, as if she was giving these questions some thought. Finally, she said, "I am as happy as I can be at this time. I married the love of my life, it has not worked out, and there is no one else for me. Do I think my husband and I can be happy together one day? Only God knows the answer to that. Now I am off to bed. Good night, Brandi."

Brandi sat for a while longer, and she said a prayer that one day Lori would be happy with the man she loved so much. Brandi turned off the lights. She stopped by her son's room, kissed him again, and went to bed.

Devin was so glad that the women were proud of her becoming an author. She knew that the book would be a hit, and she was already putting together ideas for the next one. After the charity ball, she would be going on a promotional tour for the book. She knew that the great woman herself would be calling soon. She'd had a book sent to the show, and she knew that Oprah would enjoy it.

She smiled as she envisioned sitting on the stage with Oprah. *Let me cut these lights off and go to bed, or I will sit here and dream all night,* she thought. She walked over to her husband's picture, placed a kiss on him, and said, "Good night, my darling. I love and miss you so much." Every night she told him about her day, and she could actually feel him with her. She gently caressed the picture and called it a night.

CHAPTER 10

The charity ball and fashion show were becoming the social event of the year in Atlanta. Everyone in Atlanta society was invited. Those who did not get an invitation were calling to get one. Everyone wanted to be on the A-list. Politicians, entertainers, corporate heads, the mayor and all of her top aides—if they were considered famous, they were coming into the beautifully decorated ballroom at Atlanta's convention center.

There were celebrities from all over the United States, and some from out of the country. The red carpet was being well-used. It seemed like a Hollywood event. The most famous late-night television personality was the host of the show, and Mr. Q—the world's most famous designer— was emceeing. Top singers and comedians were performing. Some of the best-known fashion models and actors in the world were modeling the clothes. No one had turned down the opportunity to help with the event.

Outside the convention center, cameras were flashing. Television stations had their cameras there to record this event. Lori and the girls had Teri, Lori's daughter-in-law, to thank for this wonderful turnout. Brandi's designs also had a tremendous effect on people wanting to be a part of this event. She was fast gaining a huge reputation in the fashion world.

After the entertainment and fashion show were over, the bidding on the clothes began—and it was intense. Items were going for thousands of dollars. A very well-known singer got into a bidding war with a famous actor on an outfit, and the singer finally got it for $25,000. Lori and the women were so excited they could hardly speak. Brandi was in awe of it all, and so grateful for her good fortune.

At the end of the event, Brandi announced that they were opening boutiques in Beverly Hills and Miami, and that New York was also on the drawing board. The crowd cheered this announcement. Next, they told the crowd about the foundation and invited audience members to help in any way they could.

The entire night was a success. The mayor of Atlanta endorsed the foundation, and she also applauded their efforts in the fight against AIDS. They had been in the limelight for only a short while, but they were carving a niche in the public eye.

The women all met in Brandi's suite after the show was over. They were happy but thoroughly exhausted. No one said anything. They just sat quietly savoring the night.

Frank and Robert were proud of their women and all they were accomplishing. The two men got a bottle of wine and cheese, served the girls, and allowed them to bask in their moment. The phones were ringing off the hook in each of the women's suites with well-wishers calling and people offering something or wanting them to do something. They took no calls, and they all stayed in one suite together. They just wanted to be close and celebrate with each other.

The next morning, the women prepared to head home. Lori rode to the airport with them in the hotel's limo and stayed until their plane took off. Teri and her law firm were making sure that the business side of the event was taken care of. That included making sure all of the money was going to the right place. They had no worries there.

There were many people Lori wanted to call and thank personally. Some would receive personal notes. Her secretary would handle all of that for her. There were quite a few that she was going to set up luncheons and dinners with. She had now been introduced to the social circle of Atlanta, and she was going to cultivate it for the good of the foundation and her fight against AIDS.

Lori's daughter was doing fine on her meds now, but it was always in the back of Lori's mind that she could lose her daughter to this disease.

She shivered as a cold feeling came over her, as she thought about her daughter and all they had gone through because of the AIDS virus. She felt so blessed that things were going good for her at this time.

Lori made an effort to change her thoughts. She only wanted to think of good things, and she was glad that only good things were happening in her life at this time. She went back to working on her list of whom she would call and invite to lunch or dinner.

Teri and her law partner were happy about the way the evening had gone. Not only did they raise a lot of money for charity, Teri was able to present Lori to the elite of the city. In addition, it showed everyone the power Teri had. Her firm had been elevated to an even higher position among Atlanta's most powerful. There were numerous calls to her office from important people wanting to meet with her and her partner.

Teri appreciated all of this, but she was a very levelheaded person. She was not easily impressed, and she was as honest as anyone on earth could be. She had very high standards for herself and her firm. She was happy for what all of this would mean to Lori's foundation, the boutiques, and the fight against AIDS. She was happy to be helping Lori find a niche for herself in Atlanta. Lori deserved all good things to happen to her. Life had not been easy for her, but she kept on making things happen in her life. That was what made Teri admire her the most—that, and the fact she had given Teri the most wonderful husband in the world.

CHAPTER 11

The next big event for Devin was her book tour. She boarded an airplane heading to New York, where she was scheduled to do book signings and appear on the leading talk shows on television and radio. She was excited and nervous. She thought, *what if no one shows up for the signings?* She had been booked at the Trump hotel. The airplane landed, and Devin felt very nervous as she left the plane.

At the terminal, she saw a uniformed chauffer holding up a sign with her name on it. She walked over to him, and he took over from there. Devin had never seen so many people moving about in one place in her life, and she felt very small and overwhelmed by it all. The chauffeur's name was Martin, and he got her luggage, escorted her to a black limo, and whisked her away from Kennedy Airport.

The city looked big and a little scary to her. At the hotel, she was escorted to the top floor to a suite that was grander than anything she had ever seen. She looked out the window, and there was New York spread out before her. She was amazed at what she saw. She knew that she was destined to be here. Her dreams were coming true.

There was a knock on her door, and Devin opened it. There stood an impressive-looking woman who introduced herself as Elizabeth Wesley. She worked for the publishing company, and she had been assigned to Devin for the New York leg of the tour. She went over the schedule: Devin would appear on the *Tonight Show* the following night. She had her first book signing at Macy's at two p.m. that afternoon.

Another knock at the door, and a hairstylist and makeup person arrived. Clothes were brought up to the room, but Devin made it clear that Brandi had designed outfits for her especially for this trip, and that was all she was going to wear.

They got started on her hair and makeup. When they had finished, she chose the outfit she was wearing from her collection from Brandi and put it on. Then they headed downstairs, where the limo was waiting to take her to the signing. Devin was so afraid that no one was going to show up, but as they drew near the store, she could see a long line of people waiting. She could not believe that those people were here to see her.

Elizabeth explained that the publisher had been doing a heavy promotional campaign for the book. The press had played up the charity ball and her connection to Brandi—and on top of that, the reviews of the book had been very good. The *New York Times* said it was one of the best books from a first-time novelist in years. As she stepped out of the limo, photographers snapped her picture and the crowd called to her.

Devin signed books until she thought her fingers would fall off. She was very exhausted at the end of the three hours she had spent in the store. The book was selling very well. *Okay, Miss Oprah*, she thought. *Pick up that phone and then my dream will have come full circle.*

Devin went back to the hotel and called the women to tell them about her day. Then she took a long hot bath and got ready for her dinner meeting with the publisher and the lawyer Teri had looking out for her in New York. Teri was her agent, and she was coming to New York the following day.

That night, Devin dined at one of the finest restaurants in New York. There were many famous people there, and they all seemed to know who she was. They kept coming over to the table exchanging pleasantries. She was thrilled but kept her cool, as if this was a normal occurrence for her. After all, she had played this role many times in front of the mirror, so she was prepared to handle all of the glamour and success. It was as if she had been grooming herself all of her life for this.

The next night she was on the *Tonight Show*, and when she heard her name being called, she walked out in a daze. She was really sitting on this stage, being interviewed. Finally, she heard Jimmy Fallon, the host, ask her, "How does it feel to have such huge success so quickly?"

She smiled and said, "I have been preparing for this all of my life, so this is not all of a sudden." It made her feel humble and proud. She knew that she was fulfilling her destiny, her purpose in life.

They talked about her association with Brandi, Lori's foundation and her association with it, and how strongly they all felt about AIDS. She told him that Lori had a daughter with AIDS, and so her feelings ran deep on helping as many people with the disease as possible and helping to prevent others from getting the disease. Overall, it was a successful night. She returned to the hotel, pinching herself all the way back to make sure she was not dreaming.

The next day, Devin had another signing. It was even more successful than the day before. She made all the rounds of the talk shows, both radio and television. Teri had come to town, and she made sure that things were negotiated in Devin's favor. Teri told her she was going to make a lot of money from the sales of the book, not to mention movies rights. Devin made it clear that she was not hurting for money, but she welcomed the fact that the book was going to increase her wealth. She wanted to donate 10 percent of all monies from the book to Lori's foundation.

Devin told Teri that she already had an idea for her second novel, and she was working on a children's book as well. There were other things she wanted to do, but for now, her plate was full. She still had to meet Miss Oprah. She was not going to give up on that dream.

Finally, it was time for Devin to leave New York. Her next book tour was in her hometown at two of the malls. Then she had to go to Atlanta for a book signing there. After that, it would be time to get busy on the next book. She had good people taking care of the spa and salon for her.

The women had not decided if they were going to add spas and salons to the other boutiques. They were still debating. If they did go ahead with the spas and salons, they would see if they could get a celebrity hairstylist to do them, someone with a fabulous reputation and top clients, like Jabot, the stylist to the stars. The new shops would cater to the rich and famous. Later on, they would do shops for women on a lower budget. All of these plans would free up Devin so she could concentrate on her writing. She was happy and in agreement.

Devin closed her eyes on the plane ride home and relived every moment she had spent in New York. Her book had hit the *New York Times* best-seller list, and that caused her popularity to shoot up. She was thanking God and her friends for inspiring her.

As soon as Devin got home and took a few breaths, it was time for the book signing at Books-A-Million in the mall near her home. Again, there were large crowds, and she accommodated everyone for pictures and signatures. Many of her old and new friends were there—and of course, the girls were too. They stayed in the background so the day could only be for Devin. They were as happy and excited as she was.

The next stop for Devin would be Atlanta. She was going to see Lori after she had finished all her commitments to the publisher for the book. She was looking forward to the downtime with her friend. They were both alone, and she felt like Lori needed some time with her. There had been no man in Devin's life since Jason had died, and she knew that Lori had not been involved with anyone since she had separated from her husband.

Devin would always love her husband, but she was beginning to feel that she needed someone in her life—someone to share the special times with, to talk with late at night and hold her close. She wondered if Lori felt the same way. Devin knew that Jason would want her to live a full life, not just exist. They had talked about what the other should do when one of them went first. Therefore, she had no guilty feelings about thinking of her life with someone else. Still, she wanted to talk to Lori. Lori would understand what she was talking about and how she felt. She was sure of that.

During her three days in Atlanta promoting the book, Devin stayed in a suite at the Ritz-Carlton Hotel. Afterward, she was free to spend some off time just doing whatever she wanted. She and Lori met for dinner in the main dining room of the hotel, just the two of them. They had agreed that there would be no business talk tonight.

Devin was seated at the table having a glass of wine when Lori came into the room. The maître d' escorted Lori to the table, and she ordered a glass of wine also. This was unusual—Lori seldom drank anything stronger than a Coke. The women exchanged pleasantries and settled in for a nice dinner.

Lori asked Devin how she was enjoying all her new fame. Devin told her it was overwhelming, but she was enjoying it. She admitted that she was lonely for male companionship. She felt like she was ready to begin again with someone. "I do not want to be rich, famous, and alone," she told her friend. Lori sat quietly, listening to Devin talk. She was so glad that this topic was being brought up.

Finally, Devin stopped talking, looked at her friend, and asked, "Lori, do you not get tired of being alone? Don't you want a man in your life?"

Lori replied, "Yes, and I'm going to contact my husband and see if there is any chance that he is willing to try and get himself together."

Before she knew it, Devin told her, "Stop wasting your time on him and get a life. He has not changed in forty years. You know it's hopeless. Why do you continue to hold on to false hope? Lori, you are a wealthy, attractive woman. Can you not see that there is still time for you to have something good with a man? Just like it was time for you to pursue your dreams in Atlanta. You do not have to marry, but you can go to dinner or a movie. Just to have someone to laugh and talk with. We all want that for you, honey. And when I say *all*, I mean your family and the girls. To see you completely happy would make all of us happy, Lori."

Lori finally said, "I know you're right, Devin. I really have hated the word *divorce*. To me, it meant failure. It's like saying that I wasted forty years of my life, and I have not been able to say that."

"Honey, you have not failed, nor have you wasted your life. You have a beautiful family from that union with Leo. You have loved and tried over and over with him. Honey, *he* failed *you*. You have nothing to be ashamed of. Give yourself a chance to be happy, Lori. God wants you to be happy, and He wants me to be happy. So girl, we need to start being happy with someone."

Devin and Lori were both near tears. Devin raised her glass of wine and said, "To our being happy."

Long after Lori had gone home and gotten into bed, she thought about the conversation she had with Devin. The next day, she filed for divorce. Then she called each of her children and explained what she had decided to do. Not even one tried to talk her out of it. She knew it was the right thing for her to do because she felt peace. There was no sadness and no looking back. She had decided to be happy.

Lori had not talked to Leo in months, but when he was served with the divorce papers, he called her. He told her he understood, and he wished her well. He wished he could have done better, but he could not, and the divorce freed him to forget. Lori felt genuine pity for him and told him they would always be friends, for he had been her first love, and they had a wonderful family together who loved both of them dearly.

When Lori called the girls and told them she was divorcing Leo, they were happy and surprised. They all wanted to know what brought on this decision. Had she met someone?

Lori laughed and said, "My therapist helped me reach this conclusion, and I know it is the right one." No one asked who the therapist was, and she did not say it was Devin. She would forever be grateful for that evening she and Devin spent together, and it made their friendship even stronger. Only Devin had the courage to speak the truth to her, and the truth set her free. A true friend loves you enough to tell you the truth in a loving way.

CHAPTER 12

It was the last Thursday of the month, and the girls were meeting at Devin's house. They'd set two p.m. as the time for their meeting. At one o'clock, Lori's taxi pulled up to the door. It was not long before Christine, Helen, Yvonne, and Brandi got there. Brandi was just coming back from a trip to France, Rome, and England. Helen had been in California working on the boutique there, which was set to open in a month. Christine had been working on some inner-city projects that had really excited her, and of course, Devin was working hard on her new novel.

Lori was working on the foundation. She had moved out of her daughter-in-law's office and set up her own office in a building downtown with a posh address in the very heart of the upscale real-estate area, with help from the mayor of Atlanta. She was busy also. However, everything stopped for all of them on the last Thursday of the month. That was when they met at Devin's house.

Yvonne had found a passion for decorating and had started taking courses. She had a real flair for design. She had been working on homes for some very important people and was planning on starting her own decorating company. All of their hobbies were launching them into fame and fortune. They were turning their passion into careers.

Brandi had some exciting news: she had met a French designer and was dating him. He had been pursuing her, and now she was no longer running. She showed the ladies a picture of him, and he was gorgeous. "He is coming to the states, and you all will meet him," she said. Brandi spent the next hour telling the women all about him and how they met.

He was very highly regarded in the fashion world, and he was very rich. Not that money mattered to her; she was making plenty. "I am just dating him," she told her friends, "and time will tell if we are meant for each other."

Helen had found the house of her dreams, and she was getting ready to buy it. She was going to hire Yvonne to decorate it. She also had met a man she was interested in. She had been doing so well marketing Laurel's that she was opening a marketing and consulting company with the boutique chain as her client as well as Brandi and Devin.

They all wanted to know about Christine's projects, and she told them she had purchase a building and converted it into a school for computer skills, parenting skills, money skills, and investment classes. There were classes on how to interview and fill out job applications as well as music classes going on there. She had famous people coming in not just to speak, but to stay for a while and give motivational talks on how to get ahead in life. She wanted all of the women to donate some time, and of course they all said yes. Whatever they could do to help, they would.

Brandi told the women that she would be spending most of the summer in France, studying and of course being with her friend. She was taking her son with her and renting a château for the summer. She thought that the ladies might want to come over and spend a few days with her. They all thought that was a great idea.

Lori said that Yvonne and Christine should invite their spouses along. Then she said, "Helen, you and I can check out the French men and see if they are as romantic as everyone says." They all laughed at that. However, it was settled that they would all come to France and also visit Italy and England.

Lori had always wanted to go to Europe, and now it was going to happen. She said, "I would like to take my granddaughters and my fifteen-year-old grandson with us. Maybe I will… or maybe I will go this time alone and take them later. But I intend to give them a trip to Europe before they start college."

Yvonne suggested that they should shop for a company plane that they all could utilize. "What a wonderful idea," Helen said. The more they thought about it, the more the idea appealed to them. Just like that, they were now in the market for their own airplane. They gave the assignment of buying the airplane to Frank and Robert, who would have it decorated with all the luxuries of home.

"What will we name the plane?" Brandi wanted to know.

"This time, the name will be Brandi's Dream," suggested Lori.

"That is perfect," Devin said. "We will have the most luxurious airplane ever."

"Well, I will drink to that," said Christine.

Then they all wanted to know if Lori had started dating anyone. Lori laughed and said, "I am not in a hurry to date, but I am prepared to accept when the right invitation comes along."

"Well, that is a complete turnaround," said Brandi. "We all need to know the name of that therapist you talked to, Lori."

Lori and Devin could not help but smile, and Lori said, "If you ever need her, I will definitely turn you on to her."

The rest of the evening was spent gossiping about people they had come to know. Who was sleeping with whom? The very rich and famous seem to live by their own codes and standards. On the other hand, some were very down-to-earth and real. The women agreed that they would stay grounded and remain friends no matter what. They went out to dinner and called it a night.

Yvonne and Robert had come a long way in their marriage since she had found out he was spending all of his time in a strip club. Of course, counseling had played a big part in saving their marriage. They now had an open and honest relationship. They enjoyed each other in every way. Robert was very proud of his beautiful wife and all of her accomplishments.

His business was very successful, and everything she and the women touched was turning into gold. Therefore, life was good. They had started talking about maybe adopting one or more children. They wanted to have a baby but had not been successful in that area. They were applying for adoption. They had not told the ladies yet. They wanted to see what would happen.

Yvonne went on Friday to help at Christine's center. She had met a young woman who had one child and was pregnant with another. She was not doing too well with this pregnancy, and she was afraid that she was not going to make it. She worried about what would happen to her children if she did not live.

Yvonne had taken an interest in this young woman and always looked for her. They began to talk, and the young woman—Marie—confided her situation to Yvonne. She had no family, and the man she was pregnant by was long gone. Her oldest child's father had been killed in a gang-related incident. There was no one for her to depend on. She was on welfare.

Marie and her child did not dress the best, but they were always neat and clean. Yvonne drove her home to her apartment in the projects and went in with her one night. Marie was feeling sick, and Yvonne wanted to make sure she would be okay. The apartment was furnished sparingly, but it was clean and neat.

There was very little food in the house. Yvonne told Marie that she was leaving to run an errand and that she would stop back on her way home. Yvonne headed to the grocery store and bought enough food to last them a while. Then she headed back to Marie's. She fixed dinner and told Marie that she wanted to assist her in any way that she could. Their friendship grew, and Yvonne adored Marie's daughter Tina.

Tina had the largest brown eyes and long thick eyelashes. Her face was heart-shaped, and she had dimples that seemed to have been cut into her jaws. Her hair was thick and long. She was a very pretty little girl, and you could tell that she had some Spanish blood. Marie did not talk about Tina's father, and there were no pictures of him around.

Marie was having complications with the pregnancy—high blood pressure and kidney problems. But she was already in love with this baby, and she wanted it to be healthy. One afternoon, Yvonne stopped by to check on them, and Marie was not feeling well at all. She had been to the clinic, and the doctors had told her she needed complete bed rest. "How can I do that?" she wondered out loud to Yvonne. "I have a two-year-old to take care of. What is going to happen to me and my child?"

Without hesitation, Yvonne said, "I am going to help you. I am moving you and Tina to my house."

Marie protested, saying that she could not do that. Yvonne was not taking no for an answer. She called Robert, and in a few hours they had Marie settled in a bedroom on the lower floor of their home.

Marie had never been inside a house like this. To her, it seemed like a castle. There were so many rooms, and the grounds were so large. The lawn was manicured, and the flowers were so colorful. There were trees everywhere.

Marie thanked God for her new friend. The housekeeper and cook were told that Marie and Tina would be staying. Yvonne told the cook about the special foods that Marie needed to have. Then Yvonne called her doctor and got a specialist for Marie.

The next day, Marie and Yvonne went to the new doctor, and after he had examined her, he told them that Marie needed to get plenty of bed rest, and he gave her strict orders concerning her diet and medications. Marie had not been taking her medications because she could not afford to pay for them. She had two more months before it would be time for delivery. The doctor expressed to Yvonne that he was worried about Marie and the shape she was in. He warned Yvonne that Marie would need to be very careful until the baby arrived.

That night, Yvonne had a talk with Robert and told him that if anything happened to Marie, she wanted to adopt both of the children. If Marie came through this all right, she wanted them to see to Marie and the kids having a better life. Robert could see that Yvonne had fallen in love with the little girl, and he knew that she cared for Marie. When he looked at his wife, he saw all the inner beauty of her soul, and at that very moment, he knew that there could never be anyone for him but Yvonne.

He was in full agreement with Yvonne concerning Marie and the children. They decided to talk with Marie and see if she would want them to become guardians over her little family. Marie listened to them, and she was so grateful that God had put Yvonne and Robert in her life. She wanted them to have the children if something happened to her. She knew her little ones would be in loving hands. She decided that she would name the baby Yvonne if it was a girl and Robert if it was a boy.

Robert called Teri and explained the situation, and Teri called a lawyer she knew near them to handle the legal end of it. Marie made a will giving Robert and Yvonne custody of the children. She also gave them her power of attorney so they could take care of any business for her and Tina. For the first time in her young life, Marie felt at peace and protected.

Two months later, Marie gave birth to a healthy baby boy. However, the delivery was hard on her. She suffered a stroke, went into a deep sleep, and never came out of it. Robert and Yvonne named the baby Robert Jr. Marie died two weeks later, never seeing her little son. Yvonne was very upset about Marie's death, and she made a vow that the children would never suffer and that she would tell them about their mother. She and Robert adopted both children and settled into family life.

The women were determined to spoil the children to death. They were forever sending them things, and when they were around there were many hugs and kisses for Tina and Robert Jr. Tina was already calling each woman "auntie," and Robert Jr. was growing up a storm. He was such a cute chubby little fellow. Robert was the proud father, and Yvonne was beaming over her two children.

Every night she thanked God for Marie, and she told Marie about the children in her prayers. She always ended by telling Marie that "they will know and love you because I will tell them about you and how much you loved them."

Yvonne had plenty of help with the kids. She had a cook and a housekeeper. She also had a nanny, but she still had plenty of hands-on time with them. She wanted the children to know that she and Robert loved them.

Her decorating firm was doing quite well, and she was very selective about her clients. She still helped Christine at the center. She would forever be grateful to the center. It was there that she had met Marie. In a way, Christine had made Yvonne's dreams of being a mother come true through her love for helping others.

She was completely thankful to God for all the things He was doing in her life. She was very devoted to her church and her family. Yvonne saw her friendship with the ladies as a divine happening. She saw Devin's house as the place where everything had started. She thought of the ripple effect Brandi had caused in all of their lives. She had thought Brandi was immoral and disgusting dancing at that club. Now she was grateful for Brandi being in her life, and she could not imagine what would have happened to her marriage and life if God had not put Brandi there.

She picked up her phone and called Brandi. When Brandi came to the phone, Yvonne said, "I just called to say thank you for being in my life, and to tell you I treasure our friendship. I love you, Brandi. You are truly my sister."

Brandi was moved by her friend's call and so happy for Yvonne and the life she was having. They spoke for a few minutes more, and they ended the conversation by saying, "See you at Devin's on Thursday."

At that moment, Tina came into the room calling, "Mommy, Mommy, come and see what I made for you!" Yvonne got up and took the little girl's hand, smiling as they went out of the room together.

Helen had been busy all morning. She was ready for a break. But she knew that the boutique in Beverly Hills was the biggest project they had ever attempted. It was so important that everything be just right and very elegant. Money was no object.

She picked up the phone and told her secretary to tell the pilot of their plane that she wanted to leave in three hours for California. It felt good to have a private plane so she could pick up and go at the drop of a hat; she could not wait to see what the boutique looked like now that everything was in place. She was going to give her final approval on the design and say, "Yes, we are ready to open," or "No, there is still work to be done." She would be staying at the Beverly Hills Hotel. The boutique was on Rodeo Drive.

Three hours later, she was in the air with her assistants. They were eating lunch that the chef had served them—steak, lobster, salad, potatoes, and the best rolls she had ever tasted. She was very pleased with the life she was living.

Helen had finally met someone who she was seeing on a regular basis, but she had decided that marriage was not for her. She did not need marriage to make her complete. Children she did want, and she had decided that she was going to adopt like Yvonne. There were plenty of children who needed someone to love and take care of them. She was going to look into adopting very soon.

She would never marry again, but she wanted someone in her life who could respect her as an individual, who cared about her dreams and wants, who could share her life without wanting to control her. The man she was dating now was a banker and very successful in his own right. They enjoyed each other's company, and they liked many of the same things, such as sports and music. He believed in giving back to the community. Therefore, he was involved in mentoring young people at Christine's center, and that was where she'd met him. She had seen him at functions before but had not spent any time getting to know him. His name was Thomas Holden, and he was a very handsome man.

The voice of the pilot brought her back to the present, saying, "Fasten your seatbelts. We are getting ready to land." She knew that a limo would be waiting to carry them to the hotel. She would see the boutique in the morning.

Helen was an early riser. She was up at six a.m., having a light breakfast of juice and toast on her balcony. The phone rang, and it was Brandi saying that she was in town and would be meeting Helen at the boutique. Brandi had flown in from France. Helen was glad that she was there. It would save them a lot of phoning back and forth.

At ten a.m., Helen was picked up by the limo and carried to the boutique. When she walked into the shop, her mouth fell open. It was like walking into a very elegant great room in a palatial home. Everything was gold and white with marble floors. It was exquisite, with high ceilings, crystal chandeliers, and paintings on the walls. There were no racks, only beautifully clothed mannequins. They had added jewelry and shoes as well as lingerie and coats to their clothing line. The women were in the process of developing their own fragrances and soon would be introducing these to their clients.

Brandi walked into the room and was overcome. This was even more than she had seen in her mind's eye. She just kept walking and touching things. It was as if she was branding every detail into her memory forever. Finally, she walked over to Helen and hugged her. She said that the people Helen had chosen to do the job had surpassed her wildest expectations.

Mr. Jordan, the designer, had won Brandi over and would design all of her boutiques. No one else would work for them, she and Helen agreed. Helen was so pleased with Mr. Jordan and his staff. It also took the responsibilities of the boutique design off of her, and she could concentrate on marketing and other aspects of the business as well as her other clients.

Brandi and Helen, after finishing with Mr. Jordan, decided to go shopping and check out some of the other high-class shops and boutiques. They went to all the fine stores and bought something in each of them. They were having all of the items sent to their hotel rooms. They ate lunch and sat at the table sipping wine and talking. Helen told Brandi about the new man in her life and that she was letting the relationship build on its own. She did not want to marry, and she didn't need any more drama in her life.

Brandi told her that her relationship with the Frenchman had been nice but that it was over and she was moving on. She told Helen that they would still work and collaborate on shows and designs, but the romance was over. They were still friends. However, the relationship had made her aware that she did want a man to share her life with. She also wanted a father figure for her son. But she knew that the Frenchman was not the right one for her.

Helen wanted to know what had happened, and Brandi told her, "His ego happened. He could not handle my success, and he wanted me to care only about what was good for him. I knew that it would not work, because I am not going to deny myself for any man's ego."

Brandi and her son were enjoying their time in France and traveling around Europe, and she was still waiting for her friends to come over. She was learning even more about design from some of the greatest designers in the world, and she was learning a lot about life and business. She wished all young women had the opportunity to travel and learn about themselves and the world before they made decisions and choices that they would have to live with forever.

Brandi had come a long way. The women did not know her whole story, and one day she was going to write about it. She never talked about her past and her family. Her parents had been ashamed of her when she started dancing. She became an embarrassment to them. She understood now how it made her mom and dad feel, but she thought they could have handled it better. It also hurt her that her sisters and brothers were not there for her.

Brandi was not ready at this time to acknowledge them. Her parents were getting up in age, and she loved them. She had to make peace with them and the rest of her family, but she was not ready to do that now. They never really knew why she had left college and changed so much. She tried to tell her mom but could not bring herself to admit that she had been gang-raped. The boy she was dating had set her up for his friends, drugged her, and allowed those dogs to have their way with her. Then he put the word out on campus that she was a whore. They told others she had been a willing partner in the goings-on that night.

She could not face life on campus after that. She left school and started dancing for a living. She became pregnant, and her baby's father mistreated her. She finally left him and started dancing again. Then she took up with a drug dealer and married him. More beatings and abuse for her and her baby. Finally, she got away from him and returned to the dancing scene.

She was amazed by the things she had done to survive and take care of her baby. She even sold drugs for a while. Now all of that was behind her. She forced herself to stop thinking about the past. It was too much to deal with. She knew that one day she would have to face that past, but not now.

Helen was calling her name. "Brandi, where did your mind go? You have not heard a word I've been saying."

Brandi smiled and said, "Sometimes things just come into your mind that take you to places you would rather not go. That is what happened to me just now. I'm back in the present now. The past is gone for the moment." They both laughed.

Helen saw the sadness in Brandi's face, and she knew that there were things that Brandi still had to deal with. Silently, she asked the good Lord to give Brandi the strength and courage to deal with the pain and handle whatever it was so she could have peace and enjoy her success.

They headed back to the hotel, for Brandi was only in town for a day. She had to return to France and finish getting her designs ready for the grand opening. Helen was headed back home to finish some things she was working on and would be back the middle of the following week, when she would stay until the grand opening. She loved Mr. Jordan and what he had done, but she still wanted to be back early. The mayor would be cutting the ribbon to welcome them to the city.

The usual press and stars would be there. Champagne would be flowing, and Brandi would unveil her new designs, including a few surprises. Brandi had a new assistant—Stacey, the young woman from the Atlanta store, was now working with Brandi and her team. Stacey was going to present some of her things that she had worked on. Stacey was very excited. They would be under the Laurel's House of Design by Brandi label. It was very unusual for a designer to let a helper share in the glory, but Brandi was willing to give this young woman an opportunity. This was very unusual in such a cutthroat business.

Everyone who worked with Brandi was amazed by how unselfish she was. She was willing to allow her staff to show their creative side. She encouraged them to spread their wings and fly. She was not afraid of anyone else's talent. Therefore, they worked hard and long for her. They were also fiercely loyal and protective, just as she was loyal and protective of them. Brandi had learned that respect and loyalty paid off. She had been treated so badly in her life that she knew how to treat others. Nonetheless, she could still be lethal if you tried to hurt her in any way.

Lori was busy with the foundation, and now that Brandi had promoted the store manager in Atlanta to her assistant, she was in the store more frequently. She wanted to put someone in charge who was already working for the boutique, but no one had shown they were ready for the job. Now she was looking for a person who could handle it.

Lori was in Rich's department store in the better women's dresses department, and she met the department head. Lori liked her instantly and was impressed by how she handled herself. Lori came back a few times and observed the young woman with customers and employees. Finally, Lori approached her and gave her a business card. She told the young woman that she would like to talk to her about a position with Laurel's House of Design. She asked the young woman to call her office for an appointment if she was interested in working with them. The young woman's name was Michelle Hyde.

Lori continued her shopping and left the store. If Michelle called her right away, then Lori would know that she was interested in hearing what they had to offer. If it took her a while, Lori would not be interested in her. A person knows when an opportunity is knocking at her door. Either she answers the knock and wins or hesitates and maybe loses a chance of a lifetime. Lori wanted decisive people working for her.

The ladies were really looking forward to the opening of the Beverly Hills boutique. The time was drawing near. The phone calls between them were getting more and more frantic as the time drew closer.

Finally, they were all on the airplane heading to California. They were more nervous than usual. They hated to admit it, but they were still in awe of some of the people who would be in attendance. A limo carried them to the Beverly Hills Hotel, where they all were staying. The hotel gave them the VIP treatment. They had to admit that they were getting used to being catered to. Sometimes they thought they were all having the same dream, and if one of them woke up it would all be over.

The grand opening of the boutique was a huge success. All of the who's who of Hollywood were there. The mayor cut the ribbon, and the fashion editor of the *Los Angeles Times* gave the boutique his blessing. There was not another shop in the area to compare with Laurel's House of Design in looks, style, and service.

The ladies were delighted by how well everything had gone. The boutiques in Miami and New York would open soon, and then they were going to hold off before they attempted anything else. They all needed to take time off and devote themselves to their own personal lives. They had qualified people in place to handle the boutiques and help with the different foundations. They were thinking of vacationing in France.

The women were once again at Devin's on a Thursday night, having their usual once-a-month get together. The topic of conversation was going to Europe and making it a family affair. Now that Yvonne had kids and Brandi's son would be there, Lori decided to take her granddaughters and grandson with her. They were old enough to appreciate the trip and be excited about seeing other countries. Helen had no children, but she was going to take her fourteen-year-old niece along. It was settled that this would be a family affair, with husbands and children invited.

After that was settled and a time for the trip had been set, the friends started finding out what was going on with each one of them. Devin announced that she had finished her second book, and it was on its way to the publisher. They all congratulated her. She also told them she had started dating and was enjoying being in the company of the opposite sex. Of course, that brought a new questions—like who, when, and what?

Devin's answer to one question in particular was that she was not sleeping with anyone. They all laughed, and Lori said, "Well, we sure wish you would have some of Christine's old man tales to tell." That really started them talking.

Helen told the women that she had decided to pursue adopting a child. She had given it lots of thought, and she knew that she wanted children but not marriage.

They were surprised that Helen wanted children; she had never said anything about it before. They were all supportive, and no one had anything negative to say. They all knew that there were many children out there who needed someone to love and care for them. Helen was interested in adopting older children.

Lori got up and hugged her and said, "You are kind, and I know that you will make a good mother to any little boy or girl."

After that, Yvonne started showing pictures of her two little darlings and telling how they were thinking of adding another one to their household. She and Robert were discussing it but had not made a decision yet.

Christine had never wanted children of her own, but she had fallen in love with Frank's grandson, and she was always fussing over Yvonne's two kids. She knew that the baby days for her were over, and it was too late for her to adopt. So she was determined to help her friends with their children and be content to be Aunt Christine.

Brandi had to miss this Thursday-night get-together; she was still in France. However, she called to let her friends know that she missed them and wished she could be there. Everything was going fine, and she was learning a lot about designs from the masters. She was happy that they had set a date for coming over to France, and she would get busy planning things for the kids and adults. She also told them that she was thinking about making France her permanent place of residence. The women weren't surprised to hear that, but they hoped she would change her mind. Brandi told them she would talk more about that when they got there.

Their lives were taking all sorts of twists and turns. They had no idea what the future would hold, but they knew that each one of them was ready for the challenge and all the changes those challenges would bring.

Lori's and Christine's foundations were helping so many people change their lives. They were both well pleased with the foundations and wanted to do even more. Lori was beginning to go out sometimes with a man friend, but she was not into dating, and she was content with an occasional dinner or social event that called for an escort. Life was good to all of them, and they felt grateful.

They continued to laugh and talk well into the night, making vacation plans and just enjoying each other's company. Finally, everyone called it a night and went to their own place.

Devin was so pleased that her second book was now being published. Her agent and publisher felt that she had another best seller on her hands. Devin felt that she had not yet scratched the surface of her talent. She still had many ideas that would make good reading. She still wanted to write that "mega book"—the one that would endure forever. She knew that she had it in her to write a book like that, and she intended to. But for the present, she was enjoying her success. The trip to France and all of the other countries she intended to see would broaden her horizons and give her more life experience.

Devin had done quite a bit of traveling lately; before that, she had never been more than two hundred miles from home. Now she was becoming a jet-setter. She thought about her son and realized that she had not been keeping in touch with him. Several of his calls she had not returned, and when she did call him, it was just to say a few words and she was gone again.

She picked up the phone and punched in Kevin's number. When he finally came to the phone, he was surprised to hear her voice and thought something must be wrong. Devin felt bad that he thought she'd only call with a problem. She told him that she was missing him and thinking about him, and she wanted them to get together before she went to Europe on vacation.

Devin told him she wanted to fly to New York to spend the weekend with him if he had the time to spare. He was so happy, and he let her know that he would like nothing better than to spend time with her. He truly missed his mother, but he was so proud of her new life. He had been concerned about how she would handle the death of his father, but she had showed great courage and determination in moving on with her life. He knew that his father was looking down on her with nothing but love and pride.

On Friday morning, Devin flew to New York. She got a suite at the Ritz-Carlton. She called her son's office and left word for him that she was in town and would be at his office around two. In the meantime, Devin had her hair done and got the usual manicure and pedicure. She was looking forward to seeing her son. Time passed quickly, and before she knew it, she was in a limo heading to Kevin's office.

Dr. Kevin Hampton was the head of the surgery department at one of the finest hospitals in New York City. He was well-known and respected in his field. He was Devin and Jason's only child, and they had both been so proud of him, both as a child and as a man. He fulfilled all of their expectations.

Jason and Kevin had been very close, and it had been hard on him to lose his father. It hurt that he was not able to say good-bye. His father's death had been quick and sudden. Kevin had not talked to him for a week before he died. Now he and his mother were going weeks without talking to each other, and he wanted that to stop.

He planned to tell her this when they met for the evening. His mother was waiting in his office when he walked in. She hugged her handsome son and told him how much she loved him and that they had to find a way to spend more time together. He told her he had been thinking the same thing. They really needed to stay in close contact—after all, it was just the two of them now. Kevin told his mother that when she went to Europe, he was going to come over for a few days. Devin jumped for joy. She would have her son joining her on her dream vacation. Wait until she let the girls know about this!

Devin and Kevin had a wonderful weekend together. He told his mother that he had not found the right person to settle down with, but he was looking, and when that person came along, he would know it, and he would go after her until she became his. This made Devin happy, to know that Kevin was interested in a wife and a family. Grandchildren, she thought, would be great. She smiled as she thought she would be the hippest grandma ever. All too soon, it was time for her to go back home. Kevin went with her to the airport to see her off and promised to see her in Europe.

All of the women were busy. Lori had luncheons and banquets to benefit the AIDS foundation, and she was happy with the Atlanta boutique. It was doing great. The young woman Lori had met at Rich's had called the same day, and two days later she was working at the boutique. Within several months, she became the manager. She was probably going to be promoted to the New York or Miami boutique soon enough. They were already grooming a person from within the shop to replace her when the time came.

Helen and Yvonne were working on packing for the trip. The joke was that Yvonne had so many people to pack for that she needed a month to get ready. Helen was trying to anticipate every situation that could come up, so she was packing for any and all possibilities. Therefore, she too needed a month to pack. That was the standing joke. Finally, they both decided to pack less and buy a lot when they arrive in Europe. They had found the perfect excuse to shop and shop.

At last, they were all in France. Yvonne and her family had rented a château. Helen and her niece were staying in another château with Devin. Lori and her grandchildren were staying in a château close to Yvonne's and Brandi's. Christine and Frank decided to stay in a hotel and have that honeymoon they had put off for so long. They would get with the others, but they really wanted to see France on their own. The girls were calling them the lovers and giving them a hard time for wanting to be alone. But of course they were happy for their friend.

The first night in Paris, they all went out to eat at a nice restaurant and enjoyed the atmosphere. Later they walked the streets, soaking up the sights and sounds of this famous city. The Eiffel Tower was more beautiful than they had imagined. The kids were amazed at what they were seeing. The people of France were so animated, talking with their hands and eyes. Devin wondered how they ever understood each other because they spoke so fast. There was a romantic sound to the words and the voices.

They went home and gave the small children to the various nannies. They allowed the older children to stay up and play games. The adults sat on the balcony of Brandi's château and talked for hours. One thing about the French was that everyone drank wine with every course of a meal, and Devin was beginning to feel the effects of sipping all evening. The ladies were laughing at her, because Devin was not a drinker at all.

Finally, Yvonne and Robert drifted off to themselves. They were walking by the lake with a full moon shining on the water. There was a small boat tied to a tree. They untied the boat and rowed out onto the lake. Yvonne laid her head in his lap, and he rowed the boat around the lake singing softly to her. It was the most romantic thing to be doing—in Paris, in a boat, with a full moon and the man you loved. Yvonne again thanked God that Brandi had caused a ripple effect that changed their life. She raised her head, gave Robert a long serious kiss, and said, "I love you with all my heart and soul."

Christine and Frank had a quiet dinner on the balcony of their suite. Then they decided to find a nice jazz club and listen to some good music. They were both jazz fans. The concierge recommended Le Duc des Lombards, a club located near their hotel. Some of the musicians were from the states. The band could really play. Christine and Frank listen to the music and sipped wine until late into the night. They walked back to the hotel hand in hand, not talking, just enjoying being together. That night, they made love as if it was the first time for them both. They fell asleep in each other's arms, happy and content.

The whole gang was having so much fun, and they were doing a lot of sightseeing and shopping, which delighted Lori's granddaughters.

Her grandson was thrilled with the way the French played soccer, and he made friends with some of the young men from the area where they were staying. He was on the soccer field a lot.

Devin's son was coming in that Friday night, and Brandi was having a dinner party for all of them at her place. The party was more to welcome Kevin than anything else. Devin appreciated that Brandi wanted to make him feel welcome. Brandi had really changed. She had become more beautiful and sophisticated. She was a softer, more loving person. The bitterness in her voice was no longer there. She was successful, rich, happy, and still very young. Devin hoped that one day Brandi would find love.

Devin had a limo pick Kevin up from the airport. They had time together before the dinner party. At eight o'clock, they went to Brandi's château. The whole gang was there, and Brandi had invited some of her new friends. The minute Kevin and Brandi met, there were sparks. He had met her before, but he did not remember her like this. She was beautiful and graceful. He could not stop looking at her. All of the women noticed that he could not take his eyes off Brandi. Brandi was pretending not to notice him, but she was smitten too, and she knew that she wanted to get to know him better.

Brandi was busy making sure that all of her guests were happy and enjoying the evening. She was still aware of Kevin, and she kept an eye on him. She wanted to make sure that he was interested in her too. At the end of the evening, he approached her and asked her to dance. She glided into his arms, and they began to dance to the slow, enjoyable sound of Barry White. He told her that he was having a good time and that he would be staying for a while, and would she be interested in showing him the sights? Brandi smiled and told him that she would like nothing better than to show him why she had fallen in love with Paris.

When the other guests went home, Kevin remained behind talking with Brandi. He was amazed that he had not paid attention to her before now. He knew who she was and that his mother was partners with her and loved her. He hadn't really liked her that much when they first met. Now he did not want to leave her side. This was the woman he had been looking for, and he was not about to lose her now that he had found her.

Devin had really enjoyed Brandi's party. However, she was thrilled over what she saw developing between Brandi and Kevin. They made a very handsome couple. Devin could already see them married and the beautiful children they would make. As Devin got ready for bed and thought of the beautiful wedding she would help Brandi plan, she knew she was jumping the gun, but it did not cause any harm to wish. She just knew that something special had happened between Kevin and Brandi that night.

Lori was tired, but the night had been good. She had enjoyed meeting all of Brandi's friends. They were all highly talented and beautiful people. She wondered if the other women had noticed the sparks flying between Brandi and Kevin. They were great-looking together. She wondered if Devin would want Brandi for a daughter-in-law. She knew that Devin loved Brandi, but would she want her to be her only son's wife? Lori thought this would be a good topic for their next session together.

Helen had looked at Kevin and thought what a handsome man he was. She would not have minded if Kevin had looked her way, but he had eyes only for Brandi. What a lucky devil that girl was. She could not wait to ask Brandi if she had fallen for him also. After that, Helen had lost interest in Kevin and looked at the other handsome men who were there. She found no one who interested her, but she still had lots of fun. This vacation was really turning out nice, and there was still a lot of time left for her to run into her Prince Charming.

Yvonne and Robert were happy as larks. This vacation idea was really turning out good for them. They were so in love, and Paris was bringing them even closer. The kids were happy and enjoying themselves as little ones will do when they are being catered to. They were receiving lots of attention from Yvonne and Robert as well as from everyone else in their group. So the vacation was working out fine for them too.

Christine and Frank had enjoyed the party and were enjoying the trip to Paris. They had not spent much time with the others, as they were really making the trip a honeymoon. The gang was giving them a hard time, teasing them, calling them old married people. However, they did not mind at all, for they were having the time of their lives being in Paris together.

They had all decided not to travel any further, just to stay in Paris and then head for home. Traveling all over Europe with children was not going to be so easy. Brandi had decided that she was going back to the states when everyone got ready to go home. She wanted to be available to pursue the relationship she and Kevin had started. So after two weeks of France, they all flew back to the United States. Each one had enjoyed the trip and felt that it was a growing experience.

CHAPTER 13

It had been six months since all of them had been in Paris together when Brandi gave each of the ladies a call saying that they had to meet on Thursday at Devin's. It was very important for all of them to be there.

Lori was glad that it was Sunday and she would have a few days before it would be time for the meeting. Brandi did not say what was going on, but it sounded like it was big. Helen called Lori to see if she knew what the story was. Lori said she did not have a clue. They wondered if Devin or Christine knew, but each said she was also in the dark. They all knew they would have to wait until Thursday to find out what was going on.

Finally, Thursday arrived. Lori came into town on Wednesday to make sure she would not miss anything. All of the women arrived at Devin's at three p.m. Brandi was not there. They sat around, talked, and tried to figure out what she wanted with them. Nearly two hours passed before she showed up. They were about ready to kill her for making them wait.

Brandi came in saying that she had a meeting that had run overtime and traffic had held her up.

"Girl, be quiet about all of that and tell us what is going on," said Helen.

"Well, ladies, I need you all to help me plan a very important event. You do not have much time, but I know that you ladies can handle it."

"What kind of charity event is it?" asked Lori.

Brandi laughed and said, "It is a wedding."

"Who is getting married?" asked Christine and Yvonne.

"I am!" said Brandi. Then Kevin came into the room, and Devin walked up to him and opened her arms to him and Brandi. They were all talking at the same time. Finally, Brandi said, "One at a time, please!"

After everyone had given her congratulations, Brandi explained, "Ladies, the wedding is going to be in a month, so you will not have much time to plan. We do not want a celebrity wedding. We want it to be elegant and romantic. Kevin feels the same way I do." Kevin stayed for a few minutes and then he left. He knew that the women were waiting on him to leave so they could really talk.

The minute Kevin closed the door, it was on. "Devin, you knew how serious this thing was getting, and you did not say a word to us!" Christine said.

"That is right, girl, that was cold of you," said Helen.

They all laughed and told Devin they were so happy that Devin would have Brandi for a daughter-in-law as well as friend and business partner. Devin added, "And I will become an instant grandmother to Brandi's son."

After Brandi had given them the inside info on how all of this came about, they began to talk about the wedding. Christine offered her house, but they all decided that the grand ballroom at the best hotel in town was the place to have the wedding.

Though Brandi had been very quiet during all of this, she spoke up and said she would really like to have a nice church wedding. She told them her first wedding had been in a courthouse. She was in jeans and a T-shirt, and he was dressed the same. There was no real love. After they got married, they went to a party and got high. He ended up with someone else for the rest of the night. They never had a decent life together.

"This time is different," Brandi said. "I love Kevin and he loves me. God and our love connects us both. I want to marry him in the church before God, because then, I know it will be forever. Kevin is it for me." She had tears of joy on her face, and the beauty of her love for Kevin was evident to all of them.

They were all drying their eyes and saying a church it would be. "Did you have a church in mind?" asked Yvonne.

Brandi said, "Before I decide on the church, I have to go back to my family and make things right. I want my mother and father there. I want my father to walk me down the aisle. I want to be married in my brother's church, and I want all of my siblings in the wedding. I want to do this right. So let me go and meet with my family, and then we will plan the wedding."

She added, "I have told Kevin my whole story. I left nothing out, and he still loves and wants me. We both want my family to become a part of my life again."

Lori was the first to speak. She said, "Brandi I am so proud of you and all that you have become. However, it took your past to get you to your present. Therefore, I am not ashamed of your past. You learned some of life's most valuable lessons and improved your life and all of ours. We all love you, honey, and we are in your corner."

Devin told her, "You will soon be my daughter and the wife of my son. I am so proud and happy to welcome you to my family. This will be the best wedding ever. You go and get your family together with you. We will begin working on the plans. Just tell us all that you want, and we will make it happen for you. We love you, honey."

Brandi thanked them all. The ladies were really feeling for her. They knew that she had not been in contact with her family for quite some time. They did not know all of the reasons, but they did know that some of it had to do with her dancing at that club. Her family did not approve of her life at all. There had to be more to it, but she had not told them all of it. They each said a prayer for Brandi and wished that the best would come out of their coming together.

Brandi went to see her parents the next morning. She was not sure that they would even want to talk to her. She had not been in contact with her family at all. Her brothers had tried to talk with her, but she had not been receptive to them. The only person in her family she had called or tried to communicate with was her sister Charity. She could not bear to look at her mother, because she knew how bad she had hurt her mother with her marriage, drugs, and dancing. Then she had kept her mother's grandson from her, and that had really hurt her mother. Her father did not have much to say about anything. When things got to be too much for him, he just tuned it all out and went into his own little world. Therefore, Brandi could not go to him, because she knew that he dealt with life's problems by drinking and going into himself.

As she drove to her parents' home, she could not help but relive the past. She did not know how she was going to approach her parents after all of this time. Finally, she turned onto the street where they lived, and she saw the white house with the beautiful manicured lawn. Her brother's wife's car was parked in front of the house. She had hoped that none of her siblings would be there. She pulled into the driveway and sat in the car, not able to move. *Get out of the car*, she kept saying to herself.

Finally, she found herself on the porch, ringing the doorbell. Her mother came to the door and peeked out of the window. When she saw Brandi, she opened the door and threw her arms around her daughter. She was hugging so tight that Brandi could hardly breathe. She just kept repeating Brandi's name repeatedly. She was planting kisses on Brandi's face saying, "I am so glad you are here."

Her father heard all of the fuss and came to the door. When he saw his wife hugging Brandi, tears came to his eyes, and he wrapped his arms around both of them. The three of them were hugging and crying. They were all trying to talk at once.

This seemed to go on forever. Finally, they got themselves together. Her mother ushered her into the house. Her father could only look at his beautiful daughter and smile.

Brandi's mother said, "I have longed for this moment for so long. I knew that you would come home to us one day. We love you, Brandi, and we never stopped. We are so proud of the way you have turned your life around. I kept you in my prayers. No matter what the past was, Brandi, you have pulled yourself up out of the bad and made your life good for you and our grandson. We have followed your every move. Your father and I have been watching you grow, and we knew that the day would come when you would want to see your family again. We love you so much, Brandi. We never gave up hope."

Brandi was so full, and she wanted to let her parents know that she was sorry for all the pain and anguish she had caused them. She wanted them to forgive her. She had been awful to them. She knew now that they were only trying to look out for her.

She talked honestly with her parents about her past and her present. Brandi said, "I have met the most wonderful man. We are going to marry. I want my family to meet him. I want to make peace with my brothers and their families. I want all of you to be a part of the wedding and our lives."

Her mother called the rest of her siblings and told them to come over—it was important. Before Brandi knew it, all of her siblings were in the room. They were so glad to see her, and none of them held the past against her. They were just glad to be a whole family again. Brandi told all of them about the wedding, and she told her oldest brother that she wanted to get married in his church, and she wanted him to marry her.

The family had long forgiven Brandi for any wrongdoings on her part, and they wanted her to know that they could have done better by her also. Therefore, they asked her to forgive them for not being there for her. They could have tried to understand what she was going through and not given up trying to reach her, but they did.

Brandi said to them, "I needed to go through things in my life to become who I am now, and I forgive you for any and all responsibilities for my foolish decisions. I do not blame my family. I loved all of you and I never stopped."

She wanted her brother James to counsel her and Kevin. James said he would be proud to marry her, and she could use the church for her wedding. He was concerned that she had become so famous that his church would not be big enough or grand enough. Brandi assured him that the church was just what she wanted for her wedding.

Now she was ready for her family to meet Kevin and the ladies who had played such a big part in her life. She told her family all about them, and they were anxious to meet these famous women. Her mom said, "Call Kevin, and I will fix a big dinner for all of us." Brandi wanted the ladies to be there also, and her mother said that would be fine.

Brandi was so happy, and she could not wait to introduce her family to Kevin and her friends. Most of all, she wanted to introduce her son to his grandparents and the rest of his family. Life was really looking grand to her at this time. She told her mother all about the ladies and how they would meet on Thursdays at Devin's to get their hair done, and how over the years they had built up this wonderful friendship. Then she explained how they had gone into business and about their various foundations.

Brandi left her mom after she had called Kevin and the ladies and told them what time to be at her parents' home. She went home and completely broke down crying. She was so thankful that her family had not stopped loving her. She was so sorry that she had let one incident change her whole life. But it was also that incident that had brought her to the place where she was now. She closed her eyes and began to think about that one night in her life.

It had happened while she was away at school. Brandi had wanted to fit in, so she was drinking and smoking at a party, and somehow she ended up in a room with a bunch of guys, and they had raped her. Repeatedly, they took turns with her. She did not know how many of them had violated her. She only knew that her boyfriend had set her up.

She remembered hearing people in the room laughing and urging the guys on. She did not know how she got back to her room. She woke up the next morning tired, sick, and in pain in her bed. She was not ever going to tell anyone what had happened to her. The frat brothers and her so-called friends told everyone that she was a ho and had volunteered to sleep with those guys. Her reputation at school was ruined.

It was all over campus. Brandi packed her things and left. Her parents had told her they were unhappy with her for leaving school, and when she refused to even discuss it with them, she was told that she could not live under their roof and not follow their rules. She was too embarrassed to tell her parents what had happened to her. How could she tell them that she had allowed herself to be put in that situation?

She left home and met others who told her she could make a lot of money dancing. Brandi thought, *Why not?* She was already damaged goods. She started dancing and being involved with drug dealers, and she even sold drugs. Her first husband was a drug dealer. She had never told her parents what had happened to her, but she told Kevin. He knew it all and she could not believe that he still loved her, but he truly did.

When she'd told Kevin, he'd cried and held her in his arms, rocking her like a baby. He told her it was all over, and he would never let anyone hurt her ever again. It was very necessary that she tell Kelvin all about her past so he could decide if he wanted to spend the rest of his life with her. She wanted to start their life together with a clean slate. She thanked the Lord that he still wanted her and that he saw only the good in her. The past was the past.

Brandi's parents, Mr. and Mrs. Wayne Martin, had been married for nearly fifty years. They had married very young. Her mom's name was Francine. On this special night, their family was complete, as all of their children were in the house.

Their three sons, James, David, and Michael, and their wives were there. Brandi and her sisters Charity, Sharon, and Michelle were there. They all met Brandi's son, Danny, for the first time. He was such a handsome little boy and the only grandson of Wayne and Francine. To top the evening off, Devin, Yvonne, Christine, Helen, and Lori, along with Robert and Frank, were there. Kevin could not keep his eyes off Brandi, and her mother kept looking at him smiling.

It was like a big family reunion. Francine was still a very good-looking woman. Brandi's father must have been a real looker in his day, because he was still a very handsome man. He and Francine had been praying for Brandi to come back to them and allow them to be a part of her life. Long before she became rich and famous, they had wanted to make amends with her. They really missed the opportunity to be a part of their grandson's life.

On this night, meeting all of Brandi's friends, they felt a sense of gratitude to the women for caring for and loving their daughter. Those women had been there for Brandi when her family could not be. They were so grateful that Brandi had found a good man like Kevin to share her life and her son. God had answered all of their prayers for her, and they were so thankful.

As the evening progressed, all of Brandi's family and friends were acting as if they had known each other forever. Brandi was overcome with joy. Kevin walked over to her, put his arms around her, and whispered in her ear, "I love you, and I knew that everything would be all right." She squeezed his arm and smiled. She had not felt this peaceful in years. She could now start her new life with Kevin because she had mended her ties with her family. Just looking at Danny's face and how he was responding to his relatives, especially his grandma and granddaddy, told her she had done the right thing.

The sun shining into Brandi's bedroom window woke her up. She turned over and smiled. This was the day that she would become Mrs. Kevin Hampton. She lay there for a minute just savoring the moment. The phone rang by her bed, and it was Kevin. "In a few hours, you will never wake up along again," he told her.

"I love you, and you have made me so happy," Brandi said to him. She hung up the phone and hurried out of bed to start getting ready for her wedding.

The wedding was to take place at the church Brandi had attended with her parents when she was a child. It was a modest brick church on a quiet street. Brandi had always felt peaceful whenever she had attended services there. Now her brother James was the pastor of the church.

The wedding was beautifully done. It was an all black-and-white wedding, small and simple, with only family and close friends. Brandi was the most beautiful bride any of them had ever seen. She and Kevin were both beaming. They had written their own vows, and the words brought tears to everyone's eyes. Brandi's son was the best man for

Kevin. After Kevin and Brandi were pronounced man and wife, they walked down the aisle with Danny as a family unit. It was breathtaking.

The reception was in the largest ballroom the Wynfrey Hotel had to offer. It was decorated in black and white also. All of their celebrity friends and the press were there. Everyone was having the time of their lives. Brandi managed to get away from the crowd and get Lori, Helen, Christine, Yvonne, and Devin in a quiet area together. She said, "I want to thank you all again and let you know how much all of you mean to me. You all have helped change my life, and Devin, you have given me the best thing anyone could give a woman—a good man to love her."

They raised their champagne glasses to toast Brandi. They wished her all the happiness in the world. Tears, hugs, and kisses were shared all around. Then they returned to the party.

Finally, it was time for Brandi and Kevin to depart. Her father embraced her and said to her, "Just be happy." Her mother could not stop crying, she was so happy for her daughter.

Brandi hugged Danny and told him to mind his grandparents. She and Kevin got into the limo and drove away.

After the reception, the women gathered once again at Devin's house. They all thought the wedding had been beautiful and that they all were getting what they wanted out of life. As they settled down and started talking, Helen announced, "I have found the baby I want to adopt. Well … she is not a baby. She is ten years old. It looks like the adoption is going to be approved. I am very happy about it." Of course, the women told her they would help and support her.

Christine was going on about her foundation and the good work that was going on because of it. Yvonne had a thousand stories to tell about her two little darlings. Devin was celebrating her third successful book, and the only thing that had not happened for her was meeting the woman herself, Ms. Oprah. That was going to happen eventually. Devin was sure of it.

Lori was very quiet. As the women were talking, Lori was going back to the beginning of everything for them: the night Brandi showed her designs and shared her idea of the boutiques. God, how their lives had changed since that night.

Lori said, "Brandi was thanking us, and we should have been thanking her. She helped to change all of our lives. Because of her, Helen, you are in business for yourself, a beautiful confident woman who is about to adopt a child. What a change in you! And you, Yvonne, you have become a loving, passionate woman to your husband, and giving those two kids all the love and care that they need. You thought Brandi was immoral, and now you love her and respect her. Because of working with Brandi, you now have your own business.

"She inspired you to act on your dream, Devin, and now you are a successful author and her mother-in-law. You have done things that you never dreamed you would do. Even you, Christine, have gotten so much out of being in business with Brandi and the friendship that you guys have. Your interest in young women finding their way comes from your relationship with Brandi and knowing some of things that she went through.

"As for me, Brandi has taught me that you are never too old to dream and act on your dreams. I feel that there is still time for me to find a person who I want to spend the rest of my life here on earth with. All of you have helped to liberate me.

"We have built boutiques, spas, salons. Wrote and publish books. Opened marketing and decorating firms. We have foundations to assist in the fight against AIDS and ignorance and poverty. I ask you ladies, are there still worlds for us to conquer? Are we still dreaming?"

The answer to both questions was a resounding yes.

"We are not through by a long shot," Lori continued. "We've got a lot more to do. Let us not forget to give credit to God who made all of this possible by putting all of us together. We have risen above all the challenges that we have faced and soared like birds with wings into our destiny. A stripper name Brandi inspired all of us to dream."

"Amen," they all said.

Brandi and Kevin had now settled into their new home with Danny. Brandi was busy getting out her new fall line for the boutiques. Even though she and Kevin were both busy people, they kept the home fires burning, spending as much time as possible with each other and Danny. Brandi had to go to France to purchase fabrics, but she hurried home as soon as she could. Her life was complete, and she could not wait to tell Kevin and Danny that there was going to be a new addition to the family. She knew that Devin would be thrilled.

Devin was starting on a new book when she got the call that she had been waiting for. Next week, she was going on the Oprah show. That was the icing on the cake. Devin stood in front of the mirror, smiled and said, "Hello, Oprah. I have been waiting on you to ask me to be on your show." Devin laughed aloud as she picked up the phone to call the women and tell them the good news.

Yes, dreams do come true. Never stop dreaming. Just ask these women.

ABOUT THE AUTHOR

Laura McClure is a retired hotel department manager. She is seventy years old. She is married to Robert McClure, and they have six children, sixteen grandchildren, and twelve great-grandchildren. She is president of the Dotes Foundation, which helps promote education about and prevention of HIV-AIDS.

She is very passionate about fighting for the rights of HIV-AIDS patients. Her daughter died from HIV-AIDS in October 2007.

She loves God, family, and friends.

Made in the USA
Lexington, KY
28 October 2014